Candy, Cauldrons, AND A Corpse

LAGUNA BAY MIDLIFE WITCH
COZY MYSTERY BOOK 1

Candy, Cauldrons, AND A Corpse

LAGUNA BAY MIDLIFE WITCH
COZY MYSTERY BOOK 1

DEANNA DRAKE

Fine Skylark Media
California

Fine Skylark Media
P.O. Box 1505
Lake Forest, California 92630

Candy, Cauldrons, and a Corpse
Laguna Bay Midlife Witch Cozy Mystery Book 1
Copyright © 2025 by DeAnna Drake
ISBN: 978-1-957691-02-2

Cover Design by Mariah Sinclair

Contents

About the Book

Candy, Cauldrons, and a Corpse

Laguna Bay Midlife Witch Cozy Mystery
Book 1
by DeAnna Drake

ele

Talk about cut-throat competition!

Boo Boudreaux's Halloween Boo-tique in offbeat Laguna Bay has its problems—a leaky roof, faulty wiring, and a talking shop cat who claims to be older than the pyramids.

One problem the place hasn't had in its forty-year history is a rival. That is, until now—when a mysterious woman opens a spooky season-themed store across the street, luring away Boo's customers and crushing her hopes of winning the town's annual Top Haunt window contest.

It's a monster-sized blow to Boo's business, but her financial troubles take a deadly turn when the contest judges find her competitor's corpse in a witch's cauldron, and no one looks guiltier than Boo.

Trying to clear her name, Boo rallies her cranky cat and her circle of eccentric friends to help her dig into the stranger's past. What they discover are troubling revelations that threaten to upend the peaceful community and expose the town's most dangerous and closely guarded secrets.

Can Boo and her mysterious, quick-witted cat unmask the real killer before Laguna Bay loses its legacy—and before she becomes the next victim?

Letter from Boo

HEY THERE, FRIEND—

I'm Boo Boudreaux. And before you ask, no, I wasn't born with that name. I picked it for myself when I was seven, after declaring Halloween the best day of the year and deciding I'd never answer to anything else. Turns out, the name suits me, as you'll soon discover.

These days, I run the Halloween Boo-tique, a little year-round shop filled with spooky delights, vintage décor, and a few oddities to keep things interesting. I share my home (and my headaches) with my younger sister, Delphine, who knows her way around a garden better than most, and with Khepeset—an ancient talking cat who once lounged in Cleopatra's palace and now sleeps on my clean laundry.

I used to read tarot cards. Was pretty good at it, too. But I don't do that anymore, and I'd really rather not discuss why.

What I will tell you is that Laguna Bay might look like your average coastal town, but that's just the cover. We're a haven for folks with... well, let's call them extraordinary complications. And while I don't consider myself the magical type anymore, Del and I help keep the town's protection spells running smoothly through the Laguna Bay Horticultural Society. It's mostly garden witches and strong tea, but it does the job.

In *Candy, Cauldrons, and a Corpse*, things in Laguna Bay take a dark turn. One body, too many secrets, and magical problems I just can't seem to shake. I didn't mean to get involved, but if there's one thing I've learned after all these years, it's this: when trouble comes knocking, it rarely leaves on its own.

So pull up a chair, pour yourself a cup of something warm, and settle in.

We've got mysteries to solve, secrets to protect, and—of course—a very opinionated cat with a few intriguing surprises of her own.

Welcome to Laguna Bay.

Warily yours,

Boo Boudreaux

WELCOME TO

LAGUNA BAY

Chapter 1

The Newcomer

"Would it have killed them to give a lady a little notice?"

Kheppy had curled into a fluffy gray ball near Petunia, my store window mannequin, which I'd dressed in black velvet, black-and-white-striped tights, and an electric blue wig beneath her witch's hat. The cat twitched her ears, so I knew she'd heard me.

"Don't pretend to be asleep. I had to clean your litter box this morning. You could at least show a little sympathy."

Her tawny eyes opened a sliver as I darted through the Boo-tique's aisles, grabbing a package of cotton spiderwebs from one rack, a couple of black rubber ravens from another, and a foam tombstone hanging on the wall. Considering my shop was a year-round Halloween specialty store, I had an advantage, but the display still needed work before the contest judges arrived to score it for the annual Laguna Bay Top Haunt Window Contest.

"It's about time you tended to that box," the cat grumbled. "It was beginning to smell."

As I muscled my armload of decorations to the front of the shop, the tombstone slipped from my grip and landed on the floor. A corner chipped off, exposing the white Styrofoam beneath the mottled gray surface. Great. Now I'd have to fix that on top of everything else.

"The litter box is your choice, not mine," I snapped at Kheppy. "If you're really older than the pyramids, as you say, you've had plenty of time to learn to use a toilet. It's not that difficult."

"Difficulty is not the issue." My little tabby companion sat up and lifted her chin to a smug angle. "I simply prefer the sand."

"I'd prefer you cleaned up after yourself. But here we are." I dropped the rest of my hoard beside her, which startled her and sent her racing to the top of the boxes of green slime I'd stacked near the witch's cauldron.

I paused, struck a match, and breathed a calming breath over my shop's protection candle—eucalyptus for clarity, sage for cleansing, lemon for good luck. The flame steadied me, but when I glanced up at Kheppy, reality rushed back. I still needed to dump all that goo into the cauldron and hook up the bubble-blowing machine. And where was Sissy? I'd sent her to the hardware store first thing this morning. She should have been back by now.

The scowl Kheppy directed at me told me she didn't care about the cauldron. Or Sissy. Or the contest. Her lips curled back, and she squealed, "Lucille Marie Boudreaux, that is not polite," sounding exactly like my poor, dearly departed mama. My heart almost stopped, which made

2

me glad my sister, Delphine, had reminded me to take my blood pressure pills at breakfast.

"You know I hate it when you do that," I muttered. Hearing my mama's old reproach was bad enough, but calling me Lucille? That was crossing a line. No one had called me that in fifty years. I was Boo, just like the sign over the door said.

The Boo-tique wasn't just a play on ghostly humor. It was my name and had been since I was old enough to correct people who tried to call me anything else.

But maybe I deserved some of Kheppy's wrath. After a lifetime of living with her, you'd think I would be used to her short temper. Or maybe some things in this world you never get used to, like living with a supposedly immortal cat who not only talks but can mimic any voice she's ever heard.

Until a few months ago, I'd thought our little ward was one of a kind. It came as a shock to my sister and me—and to Kheppy too, though she'd never admit it—to learn there was another. The extraordinary felines crossed paths while I was visiting my granddaughter, Luna, in Citrus Grove, a charming old-fashioned town about twenty miles inland. As it turns out, Kheppy's sister, Aneksi, lives with Luna's best friend, which means the cats can visit each other whenever the mood strikes.

Kheppy—short for Khepeset—has never been one for sentiment. But I'd swear that seeing her sister again stirred something ancient in her. They haven't visited as often as

I'd expected, but then again, magical cats are nothing if not stubborn. Or maybe that's just Kheppy.

Either way, I don't push.

Her secrets—which are known only to our closest friends—can feel like a burden sometimes. But mostly, they're just part of life. One secret among many in our strange, enchanted little corner of the world.

Thank goodness most people in our quiet beachside community were too busy with their own messy lives to pay attention to a woman who puttered around her Halloween shop all day talking to her gray tabby cat.

It probably never occurred to them that the cat could talk back.

"I'm sorry, Kheppy," I said as my frustration with her ebbed. "I'm frazzled. Yesterday, it was that laundry list of code violations, and today I'm ambushed with an early visit from the contest judges. If I didn't know better, I'd say Mallory is trying to make my life miserable on purpose."

"It might help if you would call her Mayor Haines instead of Mallory." Kheppy licked a white paw and ran it over her ears. Both front paws were white. Otherwise, she was gray and black from head to toe.

"Now you're just being mean." I pushed back the strands of my freshly dyed blue hair, a color inspired by Petunia's wig. I'd been coloring my natural gray for ages, but the blue was a first. In fact, anything beyond my original brunette was a first. But when I saw the box of jewel-tone blue on the store shelf, I'd chuckled because it reminded me of all the times I'd heard dismissive references to "blue-haired old ladies."

I would dare anyone to dismiss this blue-haired old—scratch that—mature woman.

Young people always think they invented rebellion, but I've been rebelling against one thing or another since before there ever was a "tik" or a "tok."

"It was merely a suggestion." Kheppy wrapped her tail around her white feet and watched me. "The woman won the election fair and quartered."

"Square. It's fair and *square*."

"If you say so."

I couldn't tell if Kheppy was being facetious or not, but I suppose it didn't matter. Mallory Haines had been a bossy micromanager since she was a teenager strutting around town with the local rich girls, and she's been micromanaging ever since. Even those bleached blond waves were the same.

She might not have taped the pink envelope to my door with "Violation" stamped in red ink, but she was the reason for the city's surprise inspection last week that found the leaks in my leaky roof and the faults in my faulty wiring.

Now, thanks to her meddling, I didn't just want to win the window contest to keep my winning streak intact—I had to win it. The two-thousand-dollar cash prize that went with first place was the only way I could afford to make the repairs before the city's deadline.

"Are you sure it was the mayor?" Kheppy hopped down from the boxes and moved closer to the window. She stared through the glass at the shop across the street, where a bike shop used to be wedged between the Scandinavian bakery and an art gallery.

I knew what she was thinking. When the bike shop closed, I had expected another art gallery to move in. They seemed to be filling all the vacancies lately.

When the for-sale sign came down and one announcing the Halloween Emporium went up, I couldn't believe it. In forty years of business, the Boo-tique had never had a local competitor, and now we had one across the street.

It didn't even appear to be one of those temporary shops that moved into empty buildings around this time of year to sell cheap costumes and décor. Those usually closed as soon as the after-Halloween liquidation sales were done. As far as I could tell, this one was permanent.

In the two weeks since the shop had opened, I hadn't had the nerve to walk inside. I wasn't above sending spies to report back, though. What I'd gleaned from those covert operations was that the newcomer had basically created my shop's evil twin. We both sold ghoulish art, decorations, party supplies, and housewares celebrating the spookiest time of the year.

What I couldn't figure out was who the woman was who ran the place. The few times I'd seen her opening the shop, she appeared to be middle-aged, wore her dark hair in a tight French twist, and dressed for a corporate boardroom—not a kitschy specialty shop. Honestly, who wore pencil skirts and four-inch heels in retail?

My trusty Birkenstocks weren't fancy, but they kept my tootsies happy, thank you very much.

I stood behind Kheppy and stared at the offensive shop. "Do you really think she could be behind it?"

"I would bet the money on it."

"I'd bet money on it," I corrected.

"Then you agree?"

It wasn't what I meant, but it didn't matter. Kheppy was right. The Halloween Emporium's window had featured a couple of run-of-the-mill ghosts, tissue paper pumpkins, and a sad excuse for a scarecrow when I left last night.

This morning, articulated skeletons, two in tuxes and two in satin gowns, sat around an upscale table covered in black spiders and cobwebs in what had to be the best afterlife dinner party tableau I'd ever seen.

"It is impressive," Kheppy added as I took it all in.

"No," I said. "It's war."

Chapter 2

Bubble and Trouble

THAT AFTERLIFE DINNER PARTY lit a fire under me. Sure, my edgy witch mannequin with her slime-filled cauldron in the creepy graveyard scene was good, if I did say so myself. I'd won with less in the past, so I expected this year's extra effort would make me a shoo-in.

Now, I wasn't so sure. I checked the shop clock again. The judges would arrive in two hours, barely enough time to improve the window.

I'd already added more webs, filled in the tombstone's white spot with a black marker, and secured the rubber ravens to the fake trees dripping with ghostly gray Spanish moss. I'd even dumped all that thick, green goo into the cauldron.

But I still needed the bubble machine to create the boiling effect. Where was Sissy anyway? I'd tried calling, but it went straight to voicemail. I'd sent a text message too, but so far, no response.

An icy chill raced through me. If she didn't get back fast, my bubbling cauldron centerpiece was going to fall flat, in more ways than one.

"You are worried," Kheppy said from her perch beside the cash register.

"Of course I'm worried. I thought I had this contest in the bag, but those skeletons across the street are stiff competition."

"But the bubbles in the slime. Will they not stop the show?"

It took me a second to realize she meant my earlier reference to the cauldron as a "showstopper."

"Not if Sissy isn't back soon. It shouldn't have taken her this long. I could have walked it in half the time."

The rear door slammed, and I could hear someone moving around in the back.

"Sissy, is that you?" I called.

"Who else would it be?" Kheppy grumbled in a low voice.

My finger flew to my lips in a silent *shh!* Our number one rule? No talking around those who weren't in the know. That had been true long before Delphine and I took over from our parents as Kheppy's primary caregivers.

Although Sissy had been working here for nearly a year and saw Kheppy almost daily, she remained blissfully unaware of the cat's peculiar quirks.

Despite the cat's eye roll as she slunk off to a sunny corner to nap, she knew it was for her own good.

"It's me! Sorry it took so long." Sissy entered, carrying a box that had to be the bubble blower. She set it on the counter next to the cash register and pushed her long ginger-blond hair off her lightly freckled, makeup-free face.

Oh, to be twenty-one again!

"Did Howard give you trouble?" I checked the box to be sure it was a waterproof model. "I told him to expect you. We discussed it last night."

"No trouble, but he had a lot of questions."

"Really? I told him exactly what I wanted, and he said he would put it on my tab. What was the problem?"

"It wasn't a problem. He wanted to know what your theme was and what materials you were using. That kind of thing. Then he wanted my advice about his window."

"He did, did he?" After all the years of calling the contest a silly waste of time, stuffy Howard Collins had finally decided to enter it himself. "What did you tell him?"

She cringed. "I didn't know what you'd want me to say, so I said nothing. Not really."

"Nothing at all?" I pressed.

"He made jack-o-lanterns to spell out his shop's name. I told him it looked nice."

"The whole name?" Laguna Bay Hardware and More was a mouthful. I couldn't imagine anyone having the patience to carve all those letters into pumpkins.

"Yeah, the whole thing. He said he carved them himself using a hand drill. He had big elastic bandages on both wrists, so I believe him."

I wasn't surprised. I left pumpkin-carving to the kids. My sixty-four-year-old wrists would require a lot more than elastic bandages to recover from something like that.

On the bright side, a window filled with carved pumpkins was no match for my witch-in-the-creepy-bayou window.

Once we got the bubble machine working and safely submerged in the cauldron, I went outside to admire its glory.

Sissy joined me. Her head tilted to one side, then the other. "It looks great."

Except it didn't sound like, "It looks great!"

It sounded like, "It looks... great?"

In my gut, I knew something was still missing.

Then it hit me. The scene needed smoky mist billowing over the ground for that extra-special creepy effect.

"Can you mind the shop for a bit?" I asked Sissy. "I need to get something."

When she agreed, I went to the office to grab my purse. As I lifted it, I could feel my phone vibrating inside. I pulled it out and saw the caller's name. Delphine.

"I can't talk now," I told my sister as I pushed through the door on my way out to the street. "I'm on my way to the hardware store."

"Do you have time before the judges arrive?"

"I know, that's why... wait, how do you know about the judges?"

"The cards told me."

I should have known.

"I turned the Judgment card this morning, followed by the Eight of Wands," she added. "You know what that means."

11

Lately, her cards spoke only in vague generalities. But judgment and swift action? That was pretty clear.

"Did they tell you anything else?" I asked.

"No, but I know you need help. I can hear it in your voice."

"What I need is to get to the store, Del. I can't talk about this now."

She kept talking. "I had an idea, and I think it's a good one. Have you considered offering the judges refreshments when they get there? I froze a dozen of the pumpkin spice cupcakes Luna brought to Sunday dinner. I could pull them out, and you could serve them. A sweet treat might sweeten your score."

"There are rules against bribing the judges," I reminded her.

"Really? I heard the woman across the street ordered a dozen chocolate eclairs from her neighbor with strict instructions to have them ready this morning."

Apparently, the cards weren't the only ones whispering in my sister's ear.

Well, if Miss Snooty-Pants with her skeleton crew didn't think sweets fell into the bribery category, I wouldn't either. "Can you get them here in time?"

"That's the thing, Boo," my sister said. "My car is still in the shop. New tires, remember?"

I didn't until she mentioned it. Sissy didn't have a car, and as much as I liked that girl, I wasn't about to give her the keys to my beloved 1971 Karmann Ghia.

Which meant Sissy would have to get the dry ice, and I would call Howard as I drove back home to get the cupcakes. Not an ideal plan, but doable.

"I'll be right there, Del. Can you put them together, so I can grab them and go?"

"Absolutely. And you forgot Kheppy's tuna on the counter. I'll add it to the bag."

"No tuna!" The words were out before I realized what I was saying. No matter where Kheppy was or what she was doing, she came running at the mention of T-U-N-A.

That's exactly what she did now. When I looked down, there she was, staring up at me.

"I am not bringing tuna back to the shop," I said as much to Delphine as to Kheppy. "It smells up the place. I don't need that, especially not today."

Kheppy meowed in her irritated, that-isn't-acceptable voice.

I pulled the phone away and glared at her. "Forget it. It's not happening."

She meowed again.

"Not this time."

Another sharp meow.

"You can eat it at home, but not here."

No meow, just a kitty version of a shrug.

I spoke into the phone. "Kheppy's coming with me. She'll eat the tuna at home."

"Oh, wonderful! I could use the company."

When I hung up, I asked Sissy to return to the hardware shop for the dry ice and hurry back, with an emphasis on "hurry."

She agreed and had already slipped out the back when I collected Kheppy, locked the front door, and ducked into my powder-blue baby, parked in front of the shop.

On most days, I could get home in ten minutes.

This, unfortunately, was not most days.

The single-lane road that wove through the foothills and separated Laguna Bay from the rest of the Southern California suburban sprawl was one of the quaint idiosyncrasies of this quiet beach town, but some days it could become clogged with heavy traffic or an accident.

Today, it had both.

I'd expected some congestion. It was the time of the morning when the nine-to-fivers were usually motoring their way toward the freeway. But I hadn't anticipated the jackknifed semi with the tire blowout that was completely blocking all lanes in both directions.

If the massive tow truck hadn't passed me in the first few minutes of the standstill, I would have abandoned the trip altogether.

But hope kept me and Kheppy in that lane.

Hope that things would get moving quickly.

Hope that the judges would appreciate homemade pumpkin spice cupcakes over ordinary chocolate eclairs.

Hope that Sissy could get that dry ice set up in case I didn't make it back before the judges showed up.

By the time traffic flowed again, I knew I was going to be late. The only question was by how much.

Delphine, that dear heart, was standing at the end of our driveway, waiting for me with the cupcakes on our prettiest platter. I didn't even have to get out of the car. She opened the passenger door, set down the platter, and scooped up Kheppy.

I was back on the road in seconds, and the traffic, thankfully, was back to normal. I told myself the judges would probably be late. When Mallory Haines had said nine a.m., it was probably an estimate. A *guess*-timate.

But no. When I turned onto Forest Avenue and saw the Boo-tique, the judges were there. Every one of them, standing around the window and clutching their clipboards.

I parked in the first spot I could find, grabbed the platter of cupcakes, and hurried toward the group with a smile and my head held high. I might have felt like I was about to lose everything, but I didn't have to show it. And all the while I was devising the story I would tell about how much I wanted to share my favorite seasonal treat. Maybe I'd include the fact that my own granddaughter had made these little darlings from scratch.

My mind was still racing when I reached the clipboard-toting bunch, which is why, when I noticed their gazes riveted on the cauldron, I thought it was a good thing. I thought the bubbling slime had captivated them, just as I'd hoped it would.

It wasn't until I could see through the window myself that I noticed it wasn't the magnificence of my bubbling slime holding their attention. It was the pair of legs dangling out of that green goo—legs that were dressed in a gray pencil skirt and two shiny black stilettos.

Chapter 3

Cupcake Catastrophe

"If you locked the shop, Ms. Boudreaux, who un-locked it?"

"How should I know?" I snapped back. "You're the detective. And stop with that Ms. business. Just call me Boo. Everyone else does."

The man, who had introduced himself as Detective Ernie Platt of the Laguna Bay Police Department, hunched beside me in his trench coat like a taller, skinnier, and younger version of Columbo as the judges and the mayor stood nearby. He was only doing his job, but he was asking me questions I couldn't answer.

I knew nothing, and that's what I was trying to tell him.

"Okay, ma'am," he said, obviously frustrated. "Tell me again what you do know."

"I walked up, saw everyone staring at my window, and when I got close enough to see that woman, I dropped the cupcakes."

"Dropped the cupcakes" made it sound like they had bounced to a soft landing, which was hardly the case. The platter had crashed onto the sidewalk, shooting ceramic shards and crumbly bits in every direction.

It made a terrible mess, but I'd ignored it completely and rushed to the shop door and found it unlocked. But I remembered locking it. Didn't I? I tried to remember as I rushed through to the back to find Sissy. She wasn't there, and the back door was locked.

No one had appeared to be in the shop, except for that dead woman.

When I explained that to the detective, he made a note in his notepad, but I could tell he still had doubts.

"What happened next?" he asked.

"Nothing. I came back out here. Mallory... I mean, the mayor was on her phone, yelling at someone, and the rest of them were cleaning up the mess on the sidewalk."

"The rest of them? You mean the contest judges?"

"Yeah." I glanced over at the librarian, the hairstylist, and the retired police volunteer, all huddled together. Their identities had been a well-guarded secret until today, but I wasn't surprised to see any of them. Each was a well-known figure in Laguna Bay and would be considered an unbiased arbiter, more or less.

Poor Helen Velchick, a retired high school teacher and now our town librarian, couldn't stop wringing her hands and muttering about never having seen a dead person before, not in person, and how she would have thought watching fifteen seasons of *CSI: Crime Scene Investigation* would have lessened the shock, but oh no, it hadn't prepared her at all.

Neal Glory, the hairstylist, patted her back and murmured obsequiously.

Thank goodness for Merle Foster, though. That big bear of a man stood beside Helen and pretended to console her, but his eagle-eyed gaze never left the detective and me. Mostly the detective.

Since I knew I could rely on Merle to protect our common interests, it comforted me to know that if anything problematic slipped out or the investigation took a troubling turn, he would be there to help me steer things back on course.

"So, the judges helped you clean up the crime scene?" the detective pressed.

"Yes. I mean, no, not the crime scene. Just the broken platter and the cupcakes." I pointed at the pile of shattered ceramic and mangled cupcakes we'd pushed against the wall until I could get a proper broom and dustpan out here.

Detective Platt scratched at his overgrown mop of black hair and shook his head like I was a lost cause.

"So, you didn't disturb the victim? Did you see anyone go near her?"

"No, sir. No one touched her. We found her exactly as you see her now."

Doubled over, face down in that cauldron full of green, still bubbling goo.

As Detective Platt chewed on the end of his pen and watched a couple of uniformed officers marking off the shop with yellow crime scene tape, Merle approached us.

"Howdy, Detective," he said in a way that made some people suspect he was a transplant from a home where the buffalo roamed, but I happened to know he was as much a Laguna Bay native as I was. He'd picked up that lingo from his box-office idol, John Wayne, in high school, and it had stuck. "I'd like to offer my assistance, seeing as you've got your hands full. We haven't met yet. The name's Merle, and you might say we're colleagues."

"Oh?" The detective slipped his pen behind his ear and extended his hand to shake. "I transferred from the Fullerton department a few weeks ago, but I haven't met everyone yet. Are you a detective too?"

Merle guffawed. "Not a detective, no, sir. I head up the department's RSVP squad."

"I see." The subtle shift in the detective's smile was unmistakable. He clearly understood that RSVP stood for a Retired and Senior Volunteer Program, and that while it was largely staffed by civilians dedicating their golden years to community service, it sometimes attracted busybodies and police wannabes.

As Detective Platt sized up Merle, I saw Sissy on the sidewalk half a block away, rushing toward us with the Styrofoam cooler of dry ice. Was she just now getting back from the hardware store?

I broke away from the detective and hurried to stop her, to protect her from seeing the horror in the shop window.

"Why are the police here?" she demanded, panic lacing her voice.

I blocked her from getting any closer. "There's been an accident. Trust me, you don't want to go over there."

"Why? What happened?" she asked.

"Was someone hurt?" A young man came up from behind her and draped his arm over her shoulder like those long, spindly legs of his were incapable of holding him upright without her.

The way Sissy gazed up at him, I knew this had to be the young man she'd been seeing the past few weeks. "Boo, this is my boyfriend, Ryan. Ryan, this is my boss, Boo Boudreaux."

Boyfriend? I didn't realize things had advanced quite that far.

Instead of reaching for my hand or smiling like a normal human, this creature muttered, "Boo Boo," and chuckled.

The wail of an approaching ambulance siren drowned out my muttered reply, which was probably for the best. When the vehicle reached the shop, police officers cleared the way for the emergency medical technicians to roll a stretcher into my shop.

Sissy's hands flew to her mouth. "Someone *is* hurt. Who is it? Who's inside?"

"It's the woman from across the street," I said as gently as I could. It occurred to me I still didn't know that woman's name. If she had died in my store, I should at least know that simple detail.

Sissy's eyebrows pulled together. "The one who opened Halloween Emporium?"

"Excuse me, Ms. Boudreaux? May we finish our conversation?"

I wasn't sure if Detective Platt really needed to speak to me or if he was trying to get away from Merle, who was droning on about his personal observations of the scene and his own theories about what might have transpired.

Either way, I still had a few questions for the detective myself.

"You just let me know if there's anything else I can help you with," Merle said as the younger man inched away. "I am at your disposal."

"I appreciate that, Mr. Foster," he said, before turning his attention to me. To his credit, he tried to hide his relief when Merle walked away. He flipped to a fresh page in his notepad. "There are a few more things I'd like to go over before I interview the other judges."

"Good, because there's something I'd like to know as well," I said. "Who is she? I mean, I don't even know the woman's name. She moved in across the street, opened a store just like mine, and now she's dead in my shop. Don't you find that a little odd?"

He frowned. "Are you saying the two of you had a business rivalry?"

Why did I have to go and open my big mouth? "I wouldn't call it a rivalry. She's only been here a couple of weeks, and to be honest, I've never spoken to her. Like I said, I don't even know her name. No one does."

His wiry eyebrows twitched. "You don't know her name?"

"No, but other people who have gone to her shop"—I omitted the fact I had urged them to do so—"they couldn't figure it out. It was like she was purposely keeping it secret."

"Why do you suppose she would do that?"

The clickety-clack of Mallory Haines's heels interrupted us.

"I'm ready to be interviewed now, Detective," she announced. "Sorry for the delay. City business waits for no man. Or woman. Or, well, anyone, I suppose. Oh, dear. Did I interrupt you, Boo?" She stepped back and stared at me for a long moment. "You know, the new hair is quite striking. It suits you."

"Thank you, Mallory," I said, even though her tone made it clear it wasn't a compliment. It didn't matter. I couldn't care less about Mallory's approval. "And you aren't interrupting. I was just telling the detective that the woman is new here, and that none of us know anything about her. I don't even know her name. Do you?"

"That is a good point, Boo. Yes, I'm glad you brought it up. Detective, you should write that down in that little book of yours." She wiggled a long, pink-lacquered fingernail in his direction. "Did you also tell him her shop was going to be the judges' next stop?"

The detective held up his hand to stop me from answering. "The victim was also participating in the window contest?"

"Absolutely! Did I not mention that before? You can see her window right there." She pointed across the street at the Halloween Emporium display.

The detective shaded his eyes for a better view of the macabre dinner party. "That's some window."

"Isn't it?" Mallory gushed. "Such a fun theme, and the use of color and materials is so creative. It's a shame to lose someone who brought such a wonderful, fresh spark to our community. An awful shame."

The detective nodded and scribbled something else on his pad. "Would you say she had a chance of winning the contest?"

"Oh, yes," Mallory said. "It's certainly the best entry." She looked at me and then back at the detective. "I mean, it's one of the best entries I've seen."

"Do you think that could have been the killer's motive? To eliminate the competition."

Mallory's perfectly tweezed eyebrows twitched on that Botox-frozen forehead of hers. "Are you suggesting another contestant might be responsible for her death?"

Why was that shrew looking at me?

With squared shoulders and my finger wagging at that weasel face of hers, I let her have it. "I know what you're implying, Mallory. But I had nothing to do with this. Nothing. At. All."

Mallory crossed her arms, pulling her plum knit blazer tight across her chest, and smirked. "Of course you didn't, Boo. I would never suggest such a thing."

The detective stepped between us. "No one is accusing anyone of anything. Ms. Boudreaux, I have no further questions at the moment. You're free to leave. But I would like another word with you, Madame Mayor, if you can spare the time."

That smug grin made me sick.

"Of course, Detective," she cooed. "I'm happy to do whatever I can to help the investigation."

As he led her further down the sidewalk, out of earshot, I didn't have to guess what they'd be discussing. As far as Mallory was concerned, I was the number one suspect, and there was a good chance Detective Platt thought so too.

Chapter 4

Back Home

"THE DETECTIVE DIDN'T COME out and say I was a suspect, but it was obviously what he was thinking." I blew a wisp of electric blue hair off my nose and dumped a teaspoon of sugar into the oolong tea my sister handed me in what we called the Kheppy mug because it had a picture of a gray tabby cat that looked just like our Kheppy alongside the phrase *Purr More, Hiss Less.*

It was my sister's not-so-subtle way of urging me to stay calm.

She'd deny it, but after living with her for most of our lives, I knew her tricks. Most of them, anyway.

The fact that I'd arrived home to find her entertaining the other three members of our gardening club, although our next scheduled meeting was still a week away, also told me she was up to something.

Did she think I needed moral support? Or did she need reinforcements?

"You don't know what he's thinking," my sister admonished before taking a sip from her own mug and squeezing herself into one of the dinette chairs. "Goodness, you didn't even know her. You had no motive. We all know that."

The others nodded and made soft reassuring noises as they held their cups. All except Jemma Tolliver, the newest and, at a sprightly forty-two years old, the youngest member of our Laguna Bay Horticultural Society.

Jemma frowned and tapped her sharply angled chin. "Delphine, you said it was the woman who opened that Halloween store across from Boo's place. Isn't that a motive?"

The way that waif of a woman yelped, I knew my sister had answered her question with a swift kick to her shin beneath the dinette table. I'd been on the receiving end of that particular move more times than I cared to admit.

"You're right, Jemma," I said before my sister could inflict any more damage on the poor woman, who was rubbing her leg beneath her paisley broomstick skirt. "The detective looks like he just graduated from the police academy, but he's no dummy. He became really interested when he found out about her shop and the fact that we were both competing in the Halloween window contest. It looks like I was trying to eliminate the competition."

It was a horribly inaccurate assessment, but even I could see how bad it looked for me.

"Sissy told her mom that woman has been nothing but trouble for you," said Opal Uttari, who had been Sissy's neighbor and friends with Sissy's mom for years. She was the reason I'd hired Sissy in the first place. So, it shouldn't have been a surprise that my friend would hear things from that quarter. Still, it felt like a knife twisting in my back. Did Sissy tell her mom everything? I made a mental note to watch what I said in the future.

"Trouble might be overstating it," I said, trying to backpedal whatever grumbling had made it to Opal's ears.

"But who was she?" asked Willa Wendall, the oldest, and arguably wisest, of our little flower power coterie. She knew more about green things than anyone I'd ever met, even Del, and she knew even more about people. Human and otherwise. "Last time we talked, you hadn't nailed down a name yet."

"I still don't know it, but not for lack of trying," I said. "That's weird, right?"

"I don't know if it's weird, but there is something about her," Willa added. "I can't put my finger on it, but it's definitely something."

"Exactly. Why was she so secretive?" I stared into my tea as if the answer might float to the steaming surface.

Willa smirked that I've-seen-it-all-and-then-some smirk of hers. "Only one reason I can think of. She had something to hide."

"Don't we all?" Delphine said. That earned a round of chuckles. "I mean, at least those of us in this room, and a few dozen outside of it. Laguna Bay has been an official sanctuary for supernaturals since the town's founding more than a hundred years ago."

Kheppy had been sleeping on the purple velvet ottoman, but that roused her. She stretched and sat up.

"Some of us were here long before the council got around to adopting the official designation."

Unlike my shop clerk and everyone else in Laguna Bay, these were my closest friends and the only people besides Del and myself who knew about Kheppy's peculiarities.

"How long have you been here, Kheppy?" Willa asked.

I leaned in, as curious to hear the answer as anyone. My family had been taking care of Kheppy for generations, but exactly how many generations had never been clear to me or, as far as I knew, anyone.

Delphine and I exchanged a look. I knew what she was thinking because I was thinking the same thing. If anyone could weasel the information out of Kheppy, it was wise old Willa.

Kheppy sat perfectly still in that pose that always reminded me of the statues of Bastet, the cat goddess revered by ancient Egyptians. For all I knew, Kheppy could be descended from that Egyptian deity. Once all eyes were upon her, though, she stretched her neck and met each gaze. "Long enough, my dears. Long enough."

"Drama queen," I muttered under my breath.

"That's all right," Willa said with her own smug grin. "It's the mysteries in life that keep things interesting."

"Exactly," Kheppy said. "Now, if you'll excuse me, the mysteries in the yard beckon."

"I hope they don't involve the neighbor's cockatoo again," I muttered as she sauntered toward the back door.

Our two-bedroom bungalow sat on half an acre at the end of a narrow dirt lane that veered off the main canyon road. Kheppy had plenty of space to roam, but she'd developed a keen interest in our nearest neighbor, a woman who lived in a converted Airstream camper, since she bought a rickety old birdcage so her ornery bird could spend time outdoors.

"Who's to say?" was the last thing I heard as Kheppy butted the screen door with her head and pushed her way into the late morning sunshine.

"What would you do without Kheppy?" Opal chuckled and sipped her tea.

"What, indeed," I groused.

"Oh, Boo," Delphine admonished gently. "You adore that little minx. Admit it."

"I admit nothing," I snapped back, but I didn't hide my smile, either. That cat could be a handful, but she was family. Before my sister made me admit anything else, I turned the tables on her. "While we're on the topic, maybe you'll tell me what everyone is doing here. Is there emergency sprout business that can't wait till the next meeting? An unauthorized seed germination? Or is this just about what happened at my shop?"

"We're concerned about you," Delphine said, confirming my suspicions. "I thought seeing some friendly faces after the, uh, that unfortunate event would help."

"The only way you can help is if you know who killed that woman," I said.

"You could try asking the cards," Delphine said.

I'd wondered how long it would take her to suggest that. She'd been trying for years to get me to pick up the deck

30

again. "How many times do I have to say it? The cards and I are done."

"Maybe you're just rusty." The way my sister winced, I knew she was expecting me to snap at her. She had good reason too. Most of our discussions on the subject ended in tears or screams or both. No matter how many times I tried, I could not make her understand I never intended to use a deck again.

As calmly and diplomatically as I could manage, I said, "Let's move on."

The others pretended to be engrossed in the craftsmanship of their mugs or the stitching of their sleeves or anything to avoid being dragged into this old argument.

"Fine," my sister said. "Then what do you plan to do?"

There it was. The question I'd been asking myself since I'd left the shop in Sissy's hands. "I don't know. Detective Doogie Howser seemed more interested in cozying up to Mallory Haines and pinning the whole thing on me. Maybe I should let him."

Delphine nearly fell out of her chair. "Why on earth would you do that?"

"Because if I don't, an investigation might turn up more than that woman's killer. You know as well as anyone what could happen if the police poke their noses around certain places in this town."

Delphine's round shoulders slumped, and she shook her head. "The shifters, the merfolk, the vampires, the psychics—we'd all be at risk. Even Kheppy."

"Even Kheppy," I agreed. "I can't let that happen."

"Of course you couldn't," Willa said. "But isn't that premature? No one is locking you up just yet. Give the police some time. They might get it right. I, for one, don't think we should sit around, waiting for the worst, when we could do something."

That's why I loved Willa. "You're absolutely right," I said. "Someone got into my shop and did this to that woman. If anyone can figure out who it was, it should be me."

"That's my girl," Willa said. "But don't think for a minute we're going to let you do it alone. Whatever you need, I'm here to help."

Opal and Jemma chimed in to add their support.

"Me too," Delphine said. "I hope that goes without saying, but I'm saying it anyway."

I looked away and blinked hard to hold back unexpected tears. "Thank you," I said when I'd composed myself. "I know I can always count on you. All of you."

"So, does anyone have a plan?" Willa asked in her typical blunt fashion.

No one seemed to. I didn't either, but as far as I was concerned, there was only one place to go when you have questions that need answers. "Who's up for a trip to the library?"

Chapter 5

The Library

As WILLA AND I walked through the Laguna Bay Public Library's sliding door, an animatronic vampire lifted his black and purple satin cape and bared his fangs. Apparently, even the book people were getting into the spirit of the season.

It was just the two of us, since Delphine had to keep an eye on a vegetable stock simmering on the stove, Jemma had to get back for the lunch rush at her gelato shop, and Opal had a granddaughter to pick up from school. I didn't mind, though. I always enjoyed Willa's company.

"I *vant* to *zuck* your blood," the vampire said in a stilted, mechanical voice as we passed by before hiding the lower part of his face beneath his cape.

"I *vant* to know who thought that was a good idea," Willa muttered through gritted teeth. "If forty years in education taught me anything, it was that we shouldn't be trying to scare kids away from libraries."

"C'mon, he's not scary. I think he's kind of cute. Not Christopher Lee cute, but he's got charm."

Willa shook her head, either in disagreement or disgust. I wasn't sure which. She dropped her voice to a whisper. "Do you think it's cute to perpetuate such horrible stereotypes? How many vampires do you know who go around threatening to suck human blood?"

It wasn't a fair question, considering only a few of them lived in Laguna Bay. "I've never heard them threaten anyone about anything, but that isn't the point. It's just for fun. I put a witch in my window with a bubbling cauldron. If that isn't a stereotype, I don't know what is. Obviously, I know witches don't all hang out in creepy forests brewing up trouble."

"No, they wait until midnight on the night of a new moon to pluck laurel leaves and willow bark for the renewal of a century-old protection spell."

"Hilarious." I suppose some people might consider our little flower power group to be witches, but I never did. We were gardeners more than anything. We seeded, we tended, and we sowed. We were caregivers. Protectors. It was true for our garden and for our supernatural community.

"Or they read tarot cards or palms or tea leaves," she added.

"Or they don't." I knew what she was doing. Like Delphine, Willa never understood why I gave up the cards.

"Good morning, ladies. Can I help you find something?"

I had been too busy feeling defensive to notice Helen Velchick sitting behind the counter. But there she was, smiling so sweetly you wouldn't know she'd witnessed that horror show in my shop just a few hours earlier.

"I'm not sure," I stammered. I looked at Willa, hoping she might step in and help, but no such luck. That smirk told me I was on my own. I took a breath and tried again. "We're here to, uh, look for... Okay, I'm just going to come out and say it. I don't know what you think happened at my shop this morning, but I didn't kill that woman."

"Okay." Helen adjusted the red-rimmed glasses sliding down her nose, but there was no hint of a smile or a frown or anything that offered any clue about what she was thinking.

"I don't want to take up your time," I continued. "Is there a reference librarian I could speak to?"

"I'm the only librarian here until two. Budget cuts."

Why couldn't they cut something we really didn't need, like parking enforcers? Or whoever taped that code violation notice to my shop door?

"I'm happy to help. What do you need?" She almost smiled.

It was now or never.

"The thing is, Helen, I'm, I mean, we're trying to find out who that woman in the cauldron was. She opened the Halloween Emporium a couple of weeks ago, which seemed odd to begin with, you know, because it's practically an exact copy of my store, and it was right across the street. I have to believe that was intentional." I was getting off track, so I took a breath and tried again. "What I'm trying to say is, I thought somebody here might be able to help us out. Is there a telephone directory or something like that?"

"We haven't had telephone directories in years, Boo," she said. "Besides, you said she's fairly new, so one of those wouldn't help, anyway. You couldn't find anything online?"

"There's no website," I said. "I searched but didn't find anything helpful."

She tapped her lips. "Strange. Did you try the county's fictitious business name database?"

"The county's fictitious what now?" I didn't know what she was talking about.

"When you opened your shop, you submitted paperwork to the county to reserve the business name, didn't you?"

Did I? That was so long ago. "I suppose I did."

"It's pretty standard. You should check there if you haven't already."

She made it sound so simple, and I was a little embarrassed to admit I was still lost. "Should we go see the county clerk for that?"

"Oh no," Helen said and waved her hand. "It's all online. Would you like me to show you?"

I was about to say that wouldn't be necessary because I'd already taken up so much of her time, but Willa stepped in.

"Would you, dear? That would be helpful." She slid a grimace in my direction and added, "Wouldn't it, Boo?"

"Yes, it would." I didn't like asking for help. Never have. I like figuring things out on my own. Apparently, Willa didn't share my go-it-alone spirit.

"No problem at all. Follow me." Helen rose and led us to the corner of the library where they had a few computers for public use. She gestured for Willa to take the seat in front of the screen, but Willa pushed me forward.

Helen leaned over my shoulder and typed a website name. Instantly, we were on the county clerk's official site. She pointed to an open field on the screen. "Type *Halloween Emporium* there, and a name should come up. If that doesn't work, go to the county assessor's page and type in the shop's street address. You might find public documents related to the lease. Let me know if you need anything else."

She patted my shoulder and walked away.

"That wasn't so difficult, was it?" Willa whispered when Helen was gone. "Left to your own devices, you'd probably still be browsing through the card catalog." She looked around. "Where is the card catalog these days?"

"When was the last time you were in a library?" I said. "It's all on computers now."

Willa frowned. "Really? No more long wooden drawers with those little index cards?"

I shook my head.

"Pity."

We agreed on that. There was something satisfying about flipping through those cards. Time marches on, though, and apparently you could not only find the

Dewey Decimal number of your favorite book online but also discover the identity of annoying business rivals.

Except the name that turned up as the owner of Halloween Emporium wasn't a person. It was a corporation. ILB Corporation, to be exact.

That was disappointing.

I searched online for the county assessor's website, and once I found it, I searched around for a way to access the database of addresses.

Nothing I tried seemed to work.

Willa must have gotten bored watching me jump from one screen to another because after a few minutes, she wandered away.

A while later, I heard her talking with Helen about the children's section and the new teen area, which got Willa reminiscing about her years as the school nurse at the local high school.

The conversation must have prompted Helen to dig up the old high school yearbooks because a few minutes later Willa came rushing back with one open in her arms.

"Look at this, Boo," she said. "You won't believe what I found."

"I can't right now," I said. "There has to be a place on this stupid site to search for an address, and I am going to find it."

"No, really, Boo," she added. "You need to see this."

"Why? Did you find a picture of me with that stupid perm? It was the seventies. Everybody had a perm."

"This is not about you."

38

Her stern tone made me instantly regret my casually dismissive comment. I lifted my fingers off the keyboard and turned to her.

She shoved the open yearbook at me.

It was a two-page spread titled *Best Friends Forever*, and amid the dozen black-and-white photographs of smiling twosomes was the woman whose identity I had been hunting for the past half hour.

In this photograph, she looked like a dark-haired Britney Spears twin with a smile that would make any Mean Girl quake in her designer boots. The caption beneath the image identified her as Isabelle Blake.

The name didn't ring any bells, but the bestie standing next to her was setting off every alarm bell, whistle, and trumpet imaginable.

It had been a long time since that face had looked as young and innocent as that fresh-faced high school student, but there was no mistaking it.

"That is who I think it is, right?" Willa said, moving her reading glasses up and down her nose as she focused on the page.

"If you think that's our mayor, then you are definitely correct."

She moved her finger to the other girl. "And that's…"

"Our mystery woman," I said.

"She doesn't seem to be a mystery to Mallory Haines, though, does she?"

"Certainly not," I replied. "In fact, they appear to know each other very well."

Chapter 6

A Better Idea

"Mayor Haines was friends with that woman?" Jemma asked as she scooped a heaping portion of pineapple gelato—relabeled in a creepy font as *pineapple poison*—plopped it in a paper cup and handed it to me.

Willa and I had walked the few blocks from the library to Jemma's adorable little shop to grab something to eat since we'd already missed lunch. On weekends, Jemma's place was usually too packed for my taste because it was close to the beach, which made it a popular stop for locals and the visiting beach crowd.

Since it was a weekday and already after lunch, we found it nearly empty. It gave us a chance to share what we'd learned at the library with Jemma.

"It would certainly appear they were friendly." Willa worked her bright orange plastic spoon into her scoop of what was usually called salted caramel gelato but was now gruesomely dubbed *cackling caramel with embalming salts*. It pushed the spirit of the holiday a bit too far, in my opinion, but to each her own.

"Why would she lie about that?" our friend asked.

It was the question I'd been asking myself since I'd laid eyes on that old yearbook photograph. I still didn't have an answer. "Your guess is as good as mine." I savored another tangy nibble of the creamy gelato and admired the white cotton webs she'd tacked to the walls, along with the flight of a hundred tiny black bats swarming around the flavor board.

She'd selected the items from my shop and asked for my advice on where to place them. It pleased me to see she'd followed my suggestions exactly. It pleased me even more that she'd decided against entering the Top Haunt window contest herself. I'd like to think I would have been a good sport if we'd been rivals, but sometimes my competitive streak got the better of me.

Luckily, that wasn't a challenge I'd have to face. At least not this year.

"Are you going to ask her about it?" Jemma was looking at me like that was the next logical step, but she didn't know Mallory Haines. She didn't have the history with that infuriating woman I had.

"It wouldn't do any good," I said. "She obviously has it out for me. I know she's the reason the code enforcers are suddenly so interested in my shop."

"These old buildings need TLC," Jemma said. "I spent a pretty penny upgrading the electrical system in here to accommodate these new display freezers."

"I don't have pretty pennies. I don't even have plain pennies with good personalities, and Mallory knows it. It doesn't even matter. She'd find fault with anything I did.

She's resented me and my shop since she was a snobby little rich girl strutting around town like she owned the place."

"Why? What did you ever do to her?" The only other customer in the shop left, so Jemma came out from behind the counter and pulled up a chair to join Willa and me at the corner bistro table.

"Who knows? It was years ago." I stabbed my spoon into my pale yellow confection.

"Was it back when you were still doing card readings in the shop?" Willa didn't take her eyes off of her cup, but I knew she was waiting for my reaction.

"It was. But that had nothing to do with it."

Willa didn't flinch, but I knew she saw through my lie.

What I wasn't going to do was open that particular can of worms. The day Mallory had waltzed into my shop and asked for a reading, every fiber in my body told me to turn her away. Why hadn't I listened to my instincts? But no, I'd given her that stupid reading, and I'd told her exactly what the cards said.

It was the last time I ever made that mistake.

Better to change the subject.

"After seeing Isabelle's high school picture, I think I remember seeing her with Mallory back then," I said. "They'd get sodas at the market and walk past my shop on their way down to the beach. If I remember correctly, Isabelle was a little wild."

Willa snorted. "Oh, come now. They were kids trying to figure out who they were and who they wanted to be. With all those hormones racing through them, it's a wonder they could keep anything straight."

"Did you know them back then too?" Jemma asked.

"Not well," Willa said.

"Were you still working at the high school then?" I asked.

"I was."

Willa was never exactly chatty, but she was being unusually tight-lipped about this. I had to wonder why.

"Do you remember anything about Isabelle?" I pressed.

"Only that she didn't finish her senior year. She transferred or maybe dropped out. I don't remember the specifics." She swallowed the last bite of her gelato and pushed back her chair. "I should be getting home. Pickles didn't get her morning walk, and she's probably tearing up the furniture by now."

Willa lived with the sweetest little pug on the planet. My friend insisted her dog could be a downright terror, but I wasn't convinced. Still, there wasn't much else we could do today anyway.

I was only halfway done with my gelato, but I pushed out my chair too. "If you have to leave, I'll walk with you."

She waved me back into my seat. "It's only a few blocks. I can manage. The weather's beautiful."

That was true. The morning clouds had burned away, leaving a bright blue sky that made the Pacific Ocean sparkle like a freshly polished diamond.

"All right," I said. "If you're sure."

She pushed the sleeves of her cable-knit sweater to her elbows and patted my shoulder. "We'll chat soon."

Jemma and I waved as our older friend stepped out and headed for home.

"Should we be worried about her?" I asked as we watched Willa through the window. "She didn't seem like her usual cheerful self."

"She's probably just tired. When my mom was in her eighties, she tired out by lunchtime. Willa's got the right idea. She needs exercise and some sunshine. It's a short walk."

"You're probably right." I savored another mouthful of the pineapple goodness.

"Are you sure you don't want to talk to the mayor about her friend? She might know who her enemies were besides..." Her sentence trailed off.

"You mean besides me?"

Her nose crinkled, and her shoulders hiked to her ears. "Sorry, but yeah."

"I told you, I don't see how it would do any good."

"But you have to do something. You said yourself, our whole community could be at stake."

"I know, but it will only make the situation worse if I give Mallory more ammunition to use against me. She's after me, not our community. She doesn't even know about the community."

At least I didn't think she did.

Jemma shook her head. "I'm worried about you. You said the detective who questioned you was named Platt,

44

right? He came into the shop this morning, and I heard him on the phone with somebody. It had to be someone in the department because he was talking about the victim. He was asking for approval to run tests on some material the coroner found under her fingernails. He thinks they might get DNA from it."

"He said that in here?" He was young, but that seemed careless, even for a rookie.

She shrugged. "It was before the crowd. The place was empty, and I might have ducked into the back, so he thought he was alone."

Attagirl, Jemma. "Did he say anything else?"

She nodded. "He got really defensive. He kept saying things like, 'The chief can't expect miracles overnight,' and 'Tell him the investigation just got started.' Whoever was on the other end of that conversation kept pushing. Finally, he said, 'We do have a suspect, but we can't bring her in until we have evidence.'"

"He said, 'bring *her* in'?"

Jemma nodded.

Obviously, he was talking about me. We both knew it.

I fished my phone out of my purse and dialed city hall.

"What are you doing?" Jemma's worry lines deepened.

I held up my index finger and continued pressing buttons until I reached a living, breathing person. "I'd like to make an appointment to see Mayor Haines, please."

Jemma leaned forward.

The pleasant voice on the other end of the line said, "I'm sorry. Mayor Haines is gone for the day."

"How about tomorrow?" I asked.

"Let me see. No, sorry. She's booked solid this week. I could schedule something for next week. Wait, next week isn't good either. Give me a moment."

"Never mind. I'll call back."

As I poked the red button on the screen to end the call, I remembered how satisfying it used to be to slam a receiver into its cradle. The good old days.

"What are you trying to do?" Jemma asked.

"If I'm about to be arrested, I need to find out what Mallory knows about Isabelle Blake sooner rather than later. I'll just camp out in front of her office until she sees me."

"I might have a better idea." There was a gleam in Jemma's eye that sparked my curiosity.

"Okay, spill it."

"I'm going to the monthly Chamber of Commerce networking breakfast tomorrow at Beachside Café."

My curiosity crashed. "Really, Jemma? I don't see how schmoozing and passing out business cards will help me."

"You didn't let me finish," she said.

"Fine. Finish."

"The mayor is scheduled to present an economic report or something like that. The point is, she's going to be there. If you're interested, you could come as my guest."

So, I could either ambush Mallory while stuffing myself with free coffee and muffins at Beachside Café or stage a one-person sit-in at city hall, which last time I checked, didn't even have a working water fountain. It was a no-brainer.

"There's one catch, though," Jemma added as though it were an afterthought.

So much for the no-brainer. I braced for whatever she was about to spring on me.

"You'll have to say you're there as a prospective new member."

"But I don't want to be a member."

"I know that, and you know that. But guests are supposed to be prospective new members. Do you think you could just say you're thinking about joining?"

"Who would I have to say it to, exactly?"

Jemma flapped her hands like a little wounded bird. A flustered, possibly-regretting-she'd-said-anything little, wounded bird. "I don't know. Whoever's there. Whoever asks."

"I'm not going to lie."

She clasped her hands in her lap, clearly agitated, closed her eyes, and took a deep breath. Then, in a strained yet calm voice, she said, "I am not asking you to lie, Boo. I'm saying just don't mention your strong opposition to joining the group."

"Even though it's a bunch of glad-handing, business-card-toting blowhards?"

"Yes."

I sensed she wanted to say more. Instead, she clamped her mouth shut and stared at me, daring me, it seemed, to give up what was probably my only chance to get a word with Mallory before it was too late.

"Fine. What time do they serve the muffins?"

Chapter 7

Sea of Suits

I AM NOT A morning person. It's bad enough I have to roll out of bed by nine, six days a week, to open the shop by ten. I'd already lost a few hours of beauty sleep the night before while preparing my Halloween window for yesterday's judging, which hadn't exactly gone as planned. So, I was less than enthusiastic about hauling myself down to Beachside Café at the crack of dawn to meet Jemma and her business chums for their early-bird networking breakfast.

I had to remind myself it was my best, maybe only, chance to confront Mallory about knowing more about that dead woman in my shop than she'd let on.

"You're wearing that?"

It wasn't the greeting I was expecting from Jemma when I walked through the café's front door at six-thirty a.m. and found her fanning out dollar-off coupons for gelato on each table.

I checked the mirrored wall behind the lectern and microphone that somebody had placed in a spot that was usually occupied by a couple of two-seater tables. The black and orange tie-dye overalls, worn over a black tee, were what I'd been planning to wear to the shop. "It's almost Halloween. What did you expect? I was going to wear a 'My Other Car is a Broom' T-shirt, but it seemed too casual."

She pressed her palms against her eyes, then went back to dispensing coupons. "It's just that people usually dress professionally for these meetings. I thought I mentioned that."

"You did. This is what I wear for my profession, so that makes it professional, right?"

Jemma didn't seem to agree.

Honestly, I didn't care if my appearance rubbed her business buddies the wrong way. I was here for one purpose, and it had nothing to do with dressing to impress. Still, I was getting some odd looks from the other folks who were milling around. They were all wearing business suits. Even Jemma had on a burgundy skirt and blouse set I'd never seen before. She looked like someone had picked her up by her slick, brunette ponytail and dipped her in a dark cherry glaze, which reminded me I was hungry.

"Where's the food?" I asked as she continued to cover every table in the place with her coupons. "I ran out of the house without eating breakfast."

"The pastries are on the back table. There's also orange juice in pitchers and coffee in the dispensers. You can help yourself."

"Don't mind if I do." I scooted off, leaving her to her task.

As I wedged myself between a guy in a light gray suit and another one in a dark gray suit to grab a delectable-looking blueberry muffin, I heard my name.

I nabbed the sweet treat and turned to see Glen Phan, the café's owner, refilling the coffee dispenser. Everyone called him Chef Glen because he always wore chef whites, even though he hadn't worked in a kitchen in years.

"I've never seen you at a chamber mixer before," he said. "I'm glad you're thinking about joining the group."

I grabbed a napkin and resisted the urge to correct him. Instead, I smiled and said, "Jemma speaks so highly of it. I didn't realize you were a member."

"I'm more than that. They voted me president last month."

I hadn't seen him that proud since the local paper had named his place the best breakfast spot in town earlier in the year. A well-deserved honor that made even more sense when you realized the café was also the only sit-down restaurant in town that served breakfast, if you didn't count the hotels, which mainly catered to tourists.

That alone earned him the business of most locals who liked to get out of the house for their first meal of the day and knew they'd always run into a neighbor or two when they walked through this door. "Congratulations. I'd raise my cup in your honor, but I'm not sure where they are."

"Here's one." He handed me a thick paper cup from behind the dispenser. "Looks like we're running low. If you'll excuse me, I'd better get more before we get started. Don't forget to put your business cards on the tables. We're here to network, after all."

"Right. Of course," I said as he waddled away. There was no point in telling him I hadn't had a business card in at least ten years, and saw no reason to start now. But I would help myself to a steaming cup of his coffee to wash down the muffin. I was adding a healthy dose of vanilla-flavored creamer and two packets of raw sugar when Jemma joined me.

"There you are." The words had an edge to them, like I'd been hiding from her, and she'd found me out. "The mayor is here. If you want to talk to her, you should do it now, before things get started."

I grabbed the coffee in one hand and that scrumptious muffin in the other and turned to face the dining room, which was becoming more crowded by the minute as more people funneled in off the street.

"The booth by the window," Jemma said when she noticed me searching.

The instant I spotted those long curtain bangs, I marched over to Mallory's table, weaving through the sea of suits. Jemma struggled to keep up, her silly high heels proving to be no match for my comfy Birkies.

"Mallory, may I have a word?" I stared down at the woman who was sitting at the center of the large, curved banquette.

I knew she'd heard me, but she continued saying whatever it was she was saying to the meek woman beside her, who was frantically taking notes on a yellow pad.

A full minute passed, but I didn't repeat myself. I waited patiently, if you considered taking two sips of coffee and one big bite of muffin while I stared her down being patient.

Finally, her head swung in my direction. She tried to push back one of those perfect curls that brushed the side of her cheek, but whatever gel, mousse, or shellac she'd applied had locked it in place. "Boo, can't you see I'm busy?"

Did she really think she could brush me off that easily? Think again, sister. I ignored her snide comment and pressed on. "I want to know why you didn't mention that the dead woman in my shop, the one who'd made my life a nightmare for weeks, just happened to be your best friend."

"My what? That's absurd. You don't know what you're talking about." She swiveled back to her meek little minion. "When we get back to the office, I'm also going to need you to fill out a requisition form for a new office chair. The one in my office is killing my back."

While she ranted about needing proper lumbar support and basic ergonomics, I set down my cup and muffin and scrolled through my phone's camera roll.

When I found the photo I'd snapped of the yearbook page, I held it out to her. "Maybe this will jog your memory. The 2001 Laguna Bay High School yearbook shows you and Isabelle Blake were, I quote, *Best Friends Forever*. I know it's been twenty-three years, but you wouldn't forget your best friend, would you? Then again, senior moments are no joke. If you're having memory lapses, maybe you should talk to a doctor."

Her lips pulled into a tight line. "It's not a memory lapse. I just couldn't see the picture clearly on that little phone of yours. Of course, I knew it was Isabelle. I didn't mention her name before because she asked me not to. I was honoring her wishes."

As if this woman knew anything about honor. "You could have said something when she turned up dead in my shop."

If her glare were a dagger, it would be plunging into my chest, *Psycho*-style.

"What did you expect me to do?" she snapped, suddenly dropping her fake-nice facade. "Senior year was a long time ago. When Izzy got herself knocked up, that was the end of our friendship. She left town, and I didn't know what happened to her until she showed up here a few weeks ago."

"Why did she come back?" I'd get to the more important question of why she'd targeted me for her special brand of harassment in a minute.

"I have no clue why she came back. You could ask the cretin who knocked her up, though. He probably knows."

"The guy is still in town?" I hadn't expected that.

"You bet he is. It's Wyatt Landon, who runs the glass-blowing shop in the old artist colony in the canyon."

"I'm familiar with him." Familiar was an understatement. I knew Wyatt better than most. His family was among the first to settle in Laguna Bay. "Have you seen him recently?"

"Are you kidding? I haven't seen that man in town in years, and I never go out to that old camp. It gives me the creeps. Everyone out there is so weird."

I wouldn't say weird, but the Landon clan could definitely be off-putting. That was true of most werewolves. Their split personalities were unpredictable, which is why they usually kept to themselves.

Last I'd heard, there were about a dozen of them living and working at that remote art colony. Most of them were Landon family members, but there were others too. Wyatt had a son from a short-lived marriage. His wife had left him when the boy was still young, and from what I'd heard, Wyatt had had his hands full raising him.

The boy must be an adult by now, but I'd never heard of Wyatt taking another mate. Delphine always knew the community gossip. She would have mentioned it.

Which made me wonder, was Wyatt the reason Isabelle Blake came back to Laguna Bay? I didn't know what that had to do with her harassing me—or why she was killed in my shop—but there was only one way to find out. I had to visit the werewolves.

Chapter 8

A New Plan

MAYOR OR NOT, I had no intention of sitting through Mallory Haines's presentation about her so-called vision for the economic revitalization of Laguna Bay. I'd had the satisfaction of telling her she was a two-faced weasel for keeping her connection to Isabelle Blake a secret, and I left with something even better. A bona fide murder suspect.

I'd never been Wyatt Landon's biggest fan, but who knew he could do something as despicable as knocking up his high school sweetheart and leaving her to fend for herself? Allegedly, anyway. We'd have to see what he said about it when I confronted him, which I planned to do as soon as I could finish my blueberry muffin and get out of here.

No point letting a perfectly good muffin go to waste.

As I said goodbye to Jemma and thanked her for getting me into the event, Mallory interrupted.

"You're not staying? I suppose I'm not surprised. All that repair work on your shop must be taking a toll. The code enforcement manager told me about all the violations they found the other day. What a shame! Please let me know if there's anything I can do to help. My door is always open to constituents in need."

"I appreciate your concern." *Yeah, right.* "It's mostly routine maintenance. Nothing to worry about." That was a big fat lie, but she wouldn't know the difference. As far as I could tell, her only job before being elected mayor was spending her rich daddy's money. "It would help, though, if you could let me know when you plan to reschedule the contest judging. Those forensics people left a mess, but I'll have the window back in shape and ready for the judges' inspection by this afternoon."

Her lip twitched. Was she suppressing a smile? "You didn't hear? I've canceled the contest. Out of respect for Isabelle."

Everything went numb. My hands, my feet, my face. Was it shock, or some crazy side effect of my new blood pressure pills? I took a deep breath to be sure I could still breathe. "I see," I said. "How does that respect Isabelle, though?" And, more importantly, how was I going to win the prize money if there was no contest?

The twinkle in Mallory's eye told me she was enjoying this. "The judges and I thought we should use the money to fund something meaningful for the city, something to honor poor Isabelle's memory. We'll still invite the community children to trick-or-treat at the downtown businesses, and I'm sure they will enjoy the windows. You understand, don't you?"

DEANNA DRAKE

"Of course." It took every ounce of my strength to push those words past my lips instead of unleashing the rant raging inside.

Her smug grin triggered an avalanche of regrets. Why hadn't I set money aside over the years for an emergency like this? Why hadn't I opened a line of credit at the bank? Why had I tossed every unrequested credit card application that ever landed in my mailbox?

Being debt-free had always felt like a badge of honor, like freedom, but now it felt like a brick wall. Even if I tried to apply for a loan now, the paperwork would take weeks. I didn't have that kind of time.

"I know it's disappointing, but part of you must be relieved," she said as she pushed past me on her way to the front of the room. The others were taking their seats, so it must be time for her speech. "Now you can focus on enjoying your golden years. Win-win."

Those trite little words were still ringing in my ears as the café's door shut behind me, and they pounded into my skull with every footstep.

By the time I reached my shop, the throbbing in my joints reminded me even Birkies couldn't dull the damage of an angry three-block walk.

Sore knees were the least of my troubles, though. Sissy, Delphine, and Kheppy were already inside. I'd asked Sissy to come early to set up the cash register, but what were Delphine and Kheppy doing here? Something had to be wrong.

58

"What happened? Did someone get hurt?" I was still breathless from the walk, so I sounded downright frantic when I rushed inside, shaking with what felt like a terrible sense of déjà vu. At least the cauldron was empty. All the green goo had been emptied into buckets by the police department's forensics team, and they'd carted it away in their crime scene van.

Sissy had washed the cauldron out, so it looked as good as new. Now, she was at the register, and Delphine and Kheppy were at the shelf of crystal balls and phrenology heads. They all jumped, alarmed by my outburst.

"No one's hurt. Good grief. You nearly gave me a heart attack," Delphine shot back.

"Then what are you doing here?" I regretted how rude that sounded, but it was difficult to be diplomatic when my heartbeat sounded like a stampede in my ears.

"You said you were going to Jemma's meeting to talk to Mallory, and I thought Sissy could use some help. I knew you'd want everything to be ready in case those contest judges came back."

My sister could be the sweetest person on the planet, and I probably didn't deserve her. I marched over, sore knees and all, and pulled her into a bear hug. "Thank you," I muttered into the silver braid she wore like a halo on top of her head.

Kheppy straightened from her perch on the shelf and meowed.

"And you, too, Khep. Of course, I mean you too."

I wasn't sure how much help Kheppy had been, but she hated to be left out of things. Considering Sissy was around, Kheppy would have had to keep her usually chatty mouth shut except for the typical kitty noises. That alone could make her irritable. So, a little extra kindness was the least I could offer.

Kheppy meowed again and settled back into her nap.

My sister pulled away and gave me a long, quizzical look. "Things didn't go well with Mallory, did they?"

She always saw right through me.

"Yes and no. What's that on your face?"

There was a dark smudge at the corner of her mouth. I pointed to the corresponding spot on my own face to help her out.

She wiped her lips, glanced at her thumb, then licked away the smudge. "Halloween fudge," she said with a smile when she saw my concern. "Sissy brought it in."

"It's in the office, if you want some," Sissy said. "I made it last night for Ryan, but he's allergic to chocolate. Can you imagine being allergic to chocolate?"

"His loss, our gain," Delphine said to Sissy, then turned back to me. "But what do you mean 'yes and no'?"

I considered reminding my sister that fudge was rarely—if ever—vegan, especially when it was covered in candy corn and orange sprinkles. But she looked so pleased with herself, I kept the comment to myself. Instead, I simply answered her question. "What I mean is, you don't need to clean up for the judges because they won't be back. The contest is off."

"What? Completely?" Delphine appeared as shocked as I was.

"The trick-or-treating event for the kids too?" Sissy asked.

"No, that's still on, but the contest is off. Which reminds me, we need to get candy. A lot of candy. Can you handle that, Sissy? Not the cheap stuff. No hard candy or knockoff brands." It had always been a source of pride that my shop offered the best trick-or-treat candy around.

Sissy pushed the register's cash drawer back into place, which made the machine ding. "Already done. But why would they get rid of the contest? People love the Top Haunt window contest."

"They think it would be disrespectful to the woman who died. They want to make some kind of donation with the prize money," I explained.

"Weren't you going to use that money to pay for repairs?" Sissy lifted the stack of pink violation citations. She thumbed through them. "The wiring. The pipes. The leak in the roof."

"Yeah, that was the plan," I said. "Now, there's a new plan."

Sissy's glance shot my way, but it was Delphine who asked, "Are you going to share it, or keep me guessing?"

I didn't exactly have a new plan, but I tried to act like I did. If I stalled long enough, something would come to me. I grasped at the first thought. "Sissy, did you get any lower bids on the work?"

"I made some calls yesterday, like you asked," she said. "A few people called back, but no one quoted anything lower than Howard's price."

Since he ran the hardware store, Howard usually had the lowest bid because he paid wholesale for his materials. Still, I'd been hopeful.

"Fine," I said. "It's not the end of the world. This is a Halloween shop, and Halloween is two days away. It's prime shopping season, so let's have the biggest sale this town has ever seen. Mark everything half off!"

It was a brilliant idea, if I said so myself. So, why did they both look so glum?

"That will completely wipe out your profit margin," Sissy said. "You'll lose money."

"I didn't say it was a perfect plan. I might lose money in the long run, but I need to pay for the repairs now. If I don't get it done, the code enforcement department will shut me down."

Delphine stepped in. "Maybe you should start with, say, fifteen or twenty percent off, and see how it goes."

"I like that idea," Sissy exclaimed.

"Wait a minute," I snapped. "Last time I checked, it was my name on the place."

They both stared at me in silence. It was more restraint than I'd shown, I had to give them that. And maybe Del had a point.

"Fine. We can start with a fifteen percent discount and see how it goes. Sissy, do we still have the sale signs we used for the after-Halloween sale last year?"

"We do, and I know exactly where they are." She disappeared into the back room.

When she was gone, I pulled Delphine closer and lowered my voice. "Mallory may be trying to sabotage my shop, but she also might have handed me a get-out-of-jail-free card."

"How so?" my sister whispered back.

"When she admitted to being high school chums with Isabelle Blake, she also mentioned the girl left mid-year because she was..." I made an exaggerated curve over my belly.

"Pregnant?" Delphine exclaimed. "That woman had a child?"

"And that's not all. The father was Wyatt Landon."

"From the art colony? Are you sure?"

Instead of answering her, I turned to greet Merle Foster, who pushed through the door with a wide, toothy grin. He pulled off his cowboy hat to wish us both a good morning.

"Did I catch you at a bad time? You two looked like you were in the middle of something important. I can come back."

"No, no," Delphine said. "Just sister things. Were you looking for anything in particular? I noticed you haven't decorated your place yet. That coin-operated fortune teller would look fantastic on your porch. Or maybe an inflatable Frankenstein monster for your yard?"

Those were the most expensive items in the shop. Not a coincidence, I'm sure.

Merle grinned sheepishly. "Those are both very good ideas, but I came by to see how you're doing, Boo. After that ordeal yesterday, I thought I'd check in and see if you could use any help."

"You don't happen to know anything about electrical wiring or plumbing, do you?" Delphine asked.

Before he could answer, I stepped in. "Del, I think Sissy needs some help looking for those signs."

"Fine. Message received." As she passed me on her way to the back room, she winked. Thank goodness she had her back to Merle.

The only thing more mortifying than my sister thinking I wanted to be alone with Merle Foster would be for him to think I wanted to be alone with him. That was not a road I wanted to travel again.

When we'd tried dating back in our twenties—which felt like a lifetime ago—it hadn't worked out. Why in the world would it work out any better now?

Despite our differences, we'd built a civil friendship, and that was good enough for me. Besides, I was too set in my ways to make room for anything more, and I was sure he felt the same.

Except that loopy grin on his face didn't seem to be saying that at all.

Could this day get any worse?

Chapter 9

Perfectly Capable

"You need a handyman, huh?" Merle asked after a silence that had already sailed well past awkward.

"No, we're fine," I said. "The shop's fine. I mean, it needs a few touch-ups here and there. Nothing major."

"Sure. It's obviously in good shape." He scanned the walls and the ceiling, where I'm sure he spotted the water stains left by the last rainstorm.

As his gaze drifted to the shelf where Kheppy was curled beside the shop candle, he reached up and scratched her between the ears before I could warn him she didn't take kindly to strangers.

Instead of the usual hiss or swipe, she leaned into his touch then settled right back to sleep beside the flickering flame.

Well, I'll be. She actually liked him.

I was still staring, trying to wrap my head around it, when he asked, "Have you got someone lined up to do the work?"

"Not exactly." Howard had given me what I was sure was a reasonable estimate. The trouble was, I still couldn't afford it. "I'll probably just do it myself."

"Really?" Those gray, wiry eyebrows shot up. "I didn't know you had plumbing and electrical experience. A woman of hidden talents."

If scouring tutorial videos on the internet and hoping for the best amounted to a hidden talent, then yes, that's what I had. Delphine had learned how to knit by watching videos. It couldn't be much different.

Instead of telling him that, I pointed to the cat. "She likes you. She rarely lets anyone besides Del or me touch her."

"What can I say? I'm a likable guy."

Was he flirting? That was the old Merle Foster I remembered. A little playful, not too serious. There might be more wrinkles around those blue eyes, but they still twinkled when he was trying to be charming.

Trying, and I had to admit, succeeding.

Knock it off, Boo. You aren't twenty-five anymore.

"She's better around our kind," I said. "But normies make her jumpy."

Normies was what some of us called humans who lacked supernatural ability. Although my only supernatural ability seemed to be the power to feed and lodge Kheppy, and occasionally clean her litter box, it had been enough to keep me in the community. At least so far.

"Sometimes they make me jumpy too. Rupert says it's something I should work on."

Rupert was Merle's spirit guide, or spirit friend, or ghost host. I wasn't clear on the proper terminology, but Merle had told me back when we dated that he sometimes saw the spirits of dead people, and Rupert was one who had stuck around.

I wasn't sure why an English traveler who had come to the area in the 1850s seeking business prospects and died in an accident involving a broken wagon wheel and too much whiskey had attached himself to Merle, but the two had been thick as thieves when Merle and I were together. That had been part of the problem. There always seemed to be three of us in that relationship, and that was one too many for me.

"If those videos don't pan out, I've done a bit of plumbing in my day. I even know a little about wiring. I'm not trying to butt in on your project, but if you want help, I'm available."

"Yes! We absolutely want your help," Delphine declared, suddenly appearing from the back room.

If she thought I didn't know she'd been eavesdropping the whole time, she was mistaken. I couldn't call her on it in front of Merle, though, and that smirk on her face told me she knew it.

"Boo, maybe you could show him the problem with the pipes in the bathroom. That's a good place to start."

She looked so pleased with herself.

"Would you mind doing it?" I was not going to play her matchmaking games. "I need to head out to the art colony."

"Couldn't that wait a little longer? We have company."

She was really laying it on thick.

Merle dropped his hand from Kheppy's head. Her eyes fluttered open for a moment but then closed again. "Are you talking about the Landon place?"

"Yeah. I need to see Wyatt."

He rubbed the hint of stubble on his chin. "You might want to avoid that place for a while."

"Why should I do that?" I shot back. It wasn't like they were zombies, or ghouls, or any of the undead with no self-control. They were just werewolves, and they had no quarrel with me. Not specifically with me, anyway.

"I probably shouldn't say anything," he said, "but when I was at the police department to get my assignments for the week, I overheard that new detective talking to the captain about that place. He said he planned to go out there this afternoon to follow up on a lead."

"What lead?"

Merle shrugged. "He didn't say."

"Did he say anything else? Has he been talking to Mallory?" They seemed like reasonable questions. So, why did Merle look so annoyed?

"What's all this about, Boo?" he said. "What aren't you telling me?"

I didn't want to tell him more than I had to, but it was clear I had to tell him something.

"I think Wyatt and the woman who died here yesterday were sweethearts in high school." I left out the pregnancy.

For all I knew, Mallory had made that up. "I want to ask him about her."

"Do you think he had something to do with why she wound up dead in your store?" Disbelief dripped from every syllable.

"Not necessarily," I snapped back, though of course that thought had occurred to me. "He might know why she came back after all these years, or why she moved in across the street, or why she was copying my business. It would be nice if someone could tell me why that woman was trying to ruin me."

"Don't you think that's a little over the top, even—"

Was he about to say, "even for you?" We'd never know because he stopped speaking the instant I folded my arms over my chest and gave him my go-ahead-I-dare-you glare.

"All I'm saying is, you shouldn't jump to conclusions." It wasn't a bad backpedal, but it was definitely a backpedal.

Delphine stepped between us. "You aren't planning to go out there alone, are you?"

Now they were ganging up on me?

"It's not a big deal," I said. "I'm just going to have a little talk with Wyatt." I hated having to explain myself to anyone. Delphine knew that.

"Going to the Landon place is always a big deal," Merle grumbled. "They don't like outsiders."

"I'm hardly an outsider. I've lived in this town longer than Wyatt has been alive."

"That's not what I mean, and you know it. They don't trust anyone who isn't their kind. It's only gotten worse

69

over the years. When was the last time you've seen any of them in town?"

It had been a while, but what difference did that make? Lots of people had their groceries delivered these days.

"They're still part of our community," I said. "I've never had a problem with Wyatt or anyone in his..." I nearly said "pack" but settled on "family." "We haven't had any trouble out there in years."

"And we want to keep it that way," Merle added. "Maybe I should go with you to make sure nothing goes haywire."

There were so many things wrong with that suggestion, it made me sputter for a full fifteen seconds before I could respond. "First, I don't need a chaperone. I am not some prissy damsel in distress who needs a big strong man to hold her hand. I am perfectly capable of doing this myself."

When he tried to interrupt me, I held up my hand to stop him. "Let me finish. I'm also not going to bring another swaggering male to his home and put him on the defensive. I've dealt with enough were—"

The sharp looks from Delphine and Merle reminded me we weren't alone. Sissy was in the back, but she might be close enough to hear. I had to be more careful.

"I have dealt with people like him before, so I know what I'm doing," I said as the final word on the matter.

Delphine didn't look convinced. Her wringing hands were a dead giveaway her anxiety was getting the better of her. "I understand what you're saying. While I agree Merle's presence might be problematic, we haven't seen any of them in months, in some cases, years. To ignore the danger of showing up unannounced and uninvited is simply foolish. So, I am going with you."

Delphine rarely put her foot down this way, and I could see the fire in her eyes. Her mind was made up.

"Fine," I relented. "You and I will go together. Wyatt has known both of us his whole life. He'll know we are no threat to him or any of them."

"I still don't like it," Merle said, but quickly added. "I won't try to stop you, but will you at least call me if things go sideways?"

All my anger at his insinuation that I needed his protection melted when he turned those sad, puppy-dog eyes on me. He really did have my best interests at heart. "All right. I'll call you."

"And you'll call to let me know when you get home?" he pressed.

"Yes, are you satisfied?" I was trying to be angry with him, but he knew I was bluffing.

"I am." He put his hat on and flicked the brim. "How about you show me that plumbing problem of yours? So, I can see what I'm up against."

Fine. If he wanted to help, I'd let him help.

"Sissy can show you," I said. I called for her, and a second later her freckled face appeared in the doorway. "Would you be a dear and show Merle where the water is leaking under the washroom sink?"

His grimace made it clear he'd expected my company, but I wanted to see Wyatt before that detective got out there and put everybody on edge.

"Sure thing, boss."

How that girl could be so chipper all the time was a mystery to me.

"Come on back, Mr. Foster. Can I get you a cup of coffee? I just brewed a fresh pot."

Merle muttered something that sounded like agreement as he disappeared into the corridor.

Delphine leaned closer to Kheppy. "Trust me. You don't want to come," she whispered.

She only pleaded that way when Kheppy was throwing a fit. What was it this time?

I joined their huddle and lowered my voice. "What's going on?"

Delphine lifted Kheppy into the crook of her arm and scratched her head, trying to appease her.

"Take me too," the cat said. "That girl puts mopey sad songs on the radio when you aren't here. I prefer your rocking roll."

Her phrasing was off, as usual, but at least she was whispering.

I stroked her head. "You mean rock and roll, but Delphine is right. You don't want to come. Weren't you listening? We're going to the art colony." I mouthed the word "werewolves."

Kheppy stiffened. "I do not care for dogs."

She could be so frustrating. "That's why you should stay here."

"No," she snapped.

Delphine snuggled Kheppy, but my sister was looking at me. "What if she stays in the car? That would be all right, wouldn't it?"

If it was two against one, I didn't stand a chance. I also didn't have time to stand around and bicker. "All right. She can come, but you're both staying in the car. No ifs, ands, or buts."

Chapter 10

Art Colony

Despite my warning, there were buts. Or, more accurately—a cat butt. Which spent the first half of the twenty-minute drive to a remote corner of the canyon in irritating proximity to my face.

"Why do you insist on standing on the backrest?" I batted Kheppy's tail away from my cheek for what must have been the tenth time since she, Delphine, and I piled into my car to make the trek out to Landon Fields Art Colony. "You have the whole back seat to yourself. Sit there. We'll both be more comfortable."

"I cannot see from down there. I prefer to be here." Her tail tickled my cheek again as she pivoted around, her four paws carefully maneuvering along the narrow tan vinyl seat, sometimes stepping onto my shoulder for balance.

"I'd better not find any claw holes," I groused.

"I know," she said and continued her precarious search for a stable spot. "You said that already."

"How about some music?" Delphine asked, reaching for the radio to drown out our bickering.

Before my sister could twist the volume knob, Kheppy launched into a spot-on impersonation of my favorite announcer: "Get your kicks at ninety-eight six, with Southland Sam on KQZE, your local source for nonstop oldies rock."

"You said it, Kheppy," Delphine said, punching the first preset button. We paused as the synthesized tune streamed through the speakers.

Half a second later, Delphine shouted, "Duran Duran!"

"Wrong. It's Kajagoogoo," I said.

When the song reached its more recognizable refrain, my sister shrugged. "You win. You always win."

"Just lucky." I smiled and pretended to be pleased, even though I suspected she'd guessed wrong on purpose because "Too Shy" had been her favorite song during her junior year of high school. She must have played it a thousand times on that little cassette player she used to wear on her hip with a pair of earphones hanging around her neck.

She was trying to lighten the mood, which I appreciated even if it took some of the fun out of the game.

We cruised in silence, listening to the tunes, until she cocked her head to the side wistfully. "Remember when KQZE used to play Elvis and the Beach Boys? Honestly, when did eighties rock become the oldies?"

"You're not going to like the answer," I said.

"Don't I know it," she said, staring out the window as we passed the art and design college and then the lumberyard. "But I don't feel old. I still feel like the same girl who camped overnight in front of Mister Music Records to buy tickets to the Eurythmics and the Thompson Twins. Remember when we did that?"

"I remember. And I can tell you this, if I ever tried to sleep on a sidewalk like that again, it would probably cripple me."

"Isn't that the truth?" She shifted her shoulders to the right, then left. "I think I might have pulled something this morning just getting out of bed." Then she laughed. "I guess it finally happened. We're officially old."

"You are not old," Kheppy said in her sweet, if overly formal voice. "When you have seen kingdoms rise and fall, then you may consider yourself old."

"How old are you, Kheppy?" Delphine asked. It was one of the questions we occasionally asked that, even after all these years, had never received a straight answer.

"Old? Are you suggesting I am old?" The cat lifted her chin in smug defiance.

Score another one for Kheppy.

"No one is old," I said. "They say age is a state of mind, and my state of mind is just fine, thank you."

My sister gave me a look that said that was wishful thinking, but I didn't care, especially on a beautiful day like this. Why argue about silly things when the sun was out and the summer-like heat wave had finally given way to something that felt more like fall? It was perfect Halloween weather.

It was so nice, I could almost forget a woman had died in my shop the day before, that I was still a murder suspect, and that the police investigation might possibly peel away the carefully crafted veil of secrecy that protected our little supernatural community.

When I turned off the main road onto the gravel path that offered the only access in and out of the Landons' property, a sharp dip jolted us out of our eighties, synthesizer-fueled reverie and sent Kheppy tumbling from the top of my backrest into Delphine's lap.

"That was a near one," she muttered when she regained her footing.

"Close one," I corrected.

"That is what I said," she snapped back.

I wasn't going to argue. Mostly because my car's meager fifteen-inch wheels wouldn't survive another bump in the road like that, so I watched the gravel intently, searching for and steering around anything that appeared hazardous.

Although Landon Drive was the official name of this twisty canyon road, locals had been calling it Deadman's Curve, after the old Jan and Dean movie, ever since a woman from the art colony was killed in a hit-and-run accident.

That had been ages ago, but I still thought of that tragedy every time I traveled this way. A somber reminder to drive safely.

Maybe that's why my eyes were so glued to the road I didn't even notice we weren't the art colony's only visitors until Delphine whispered an ominous "Uh-oh" behind her fingers.

In front of us, two black-and-white squad cars were parked near the main building, which housed a gallery and working space for the resident artists. At the door were three uniformed officers joined by what had to be Detective Ernie Platt. Who else would wear a trench coat on a day as sunny as this?

Staring at the law enforcers from the doorway in a ratty pair of denim overalls, a faded black T-shirt, and a pair of protective glasses pushed to the top of his mop of salt-and-pepper hair was Wyatt Landon, slick with sweat, dirt, and decades of contempt.

"Looks like we're too late," Delphine said. "Wyatt's already got company."

About that time, the crunch of gravel beneath my tires alerted the group to our approach. I stopped well behind the squad cars and killed the engine.

Delphine and Kheppy stared at me.

"What are you doing?" My sister obviously had expected me to loop around and leave.

"The detective has his handcuffs out," I said. "I think he's going to arrest Wyatt."

"Of course he is," she wailed. "You don't dangle handcuffs in front of somebody unless you mean it. But that's his business, not ours."

I didn't agree. When I unlatched my seatbelt, my sister shook her head. "No, no, no. You are not getting into the middle of this." She jabbed her index finger at the group as if she were poking somebody in the eye.

"I have to speak to him," I said as reasonably as I could. "I have to see what's what."

"What's what is you're lucky you're not the one getting a visit from that pair of handcuffs," she cried. "If you meddle, you can bet you'll be next on the list."

There was no way to convince her this was a good plan, so I didn't try. I opened the car door and stepped out, despite her badgering.

"It'll only take a minute. Stay here," I said through my partly rolled-down window, which had been locked in that position since the handle broke last month.

As I marched toward Wyatt and the police, my sister was still yelling, and I was still ignoring her. I was focused on Wyatt and the detective, both of whom were now watching me. The detective with bald fury, Wyatt with something closer to amusement.

At least someone was enjoying this.

"I advise you to get back in your car and leave, Ms. Boudreaux," Detective Platt warned as I approached.

"C'mon, Detective," I said with a smile. "How many times do I have to tell you? It's Boo. Right, Wyatt?"

"That's right," Wyatt drawled, as if this was a friendly visit on a regular Wednesday.

"You're new here, Detective," I said. "But Wyatt and I go way back, don't we? I knew his parents. I went to his wedding, I've seen him raise a fine son, mostly on his own, and I've seen him turn what used to be a struggling string-bean farm into a thriving enterprise for—what is it now, Wyatt? Eight, ten artists living and working on the premises?"

"Twelve as of last month," Wyatt corrected.

The way he looked at me, I could see he was as puzzled as the detective about my intentions. Wyatt and I hadn't always gotten along, and I suspected I might be looking into the smirking face of a killer, but the last thing I wanted for our community was for Wyatt Landon to be hauled away by the police before I could remind him of the damage he could do to his pack—and to every supernatural resident in Laguna Bay.

If he said the wrong thing, he could undo all the work so many of us had done over the years to create this sanctuary. There would be no going back. We'd have to leave, and for some of us, this place was the only home we'd ever known.

All I needed was a few private words with Wyatt to remind him of what was at stake.

"Boo, if you don't leave this minute, I will put you in the back of one of these patrol cars, and we will discuss it down at the station after I book you for interfering in a police investigation."

I could tell by the flare of the detective's nostrils that he wasn't kidding. Still, I had to do what I had to do.

"Could I just have a word with Wyatt, Detective? Two minutes. That's all I ask."

It was a reasonable request.

Detective Platt apparently didn't agree.

"Whatever you have to say to Mr. Landon will have to wait until tomorrow. Visiting hours at the jail begin at eight a.m. Speak to him then. Unless you would like us to take you into custody as well."

When he motioned to an officer to arrest me, I backed away.

"Fine," I said. "I'm going."

"Good choice, Boo," the detective said as I left.

"I was too late," I said after I trudged down the hill and slid back behind the wheel. "I should have gotten here before the police showed up. Now they won't let me speak to him until tomorrow."

"That's cutting it close." Delphine bit her lower lip. "It'll be a full moon in a couple of days. Remember?"

How could I forget? It was the first time Halloween had fallen on a full moon in years. But what were the chances Wyatt would be released before that?

If he were as guilty as I suspected, I didn't think those chances were good at all.

Even Kheppy seemed nervous as she paced circles on Delphine's lap.

If I had to guess, our situation had just gone from bad to the absolute worst.

Chapter 11

In the Cards

"I'm out of options." I didn't expect a response from Delphine or Kheppy as I turned the car back onto the main road and headed toward home, leaving Wyatt, the detective, and what was left of my plan to save our community from ruin in the rearview mirror.

They had been waiting for me to break the silence, though, as we rumbled along to the engine's guttural rhythm. No Kheppy impersonations. No eighties synth rock. No laughter or conversation.

All we'd had since departing the Landons' compound was taut, brittle tension.

"Give it some time," my sister said as I turned onto our lane and passed the neighbor's trailer on our way to our own single-story home. "We'll think of something. We always do."

Always the optimist.

I couldn't muster even vague agreement, just a half-hearted shrug.

Once we were inside and I'd pushed the front door closed behind us, Kheppy hopped down from my sister's embrace and brushed against my ankles. "I appreciate the sentiment, Khep, but I think I'm going to lie down. I'm tired."

"What about the shop?" Delphine asked.

"I'm sure Sissy can handle things. She's a bright girl." I knew it was a cop-out. The truth was, I didn't want to face Sissy or Merle or anyone after my dismal failure at Landon Fields. Not yet.

Delphine didn't say it, but I knew she understood. She'd let me crawl back into bed to lick my emotional wounds for a little while.

"Let's try something first," Delphine said.

Apparently, I was wrong.

When she grabbed the velvet drawstring bag that held her tarot deck off the bookcase and pulled up a seat at our dinette table, I knew what she had in mind.

"Not this again, Del." I rubbed the ache brewing at my temple. "I am not going to ask the cards."

"I understand that." She pulled the deck out of the bag and shuffled it three times. "You don't have to ask them anything. Let's just see what they have to say to me."

"I'm not interested," I said. "Besides, I should probably get to the shop."

"You said it yourself. Sissy is quite capable on her own." My sister cut the deck several times and put it on the table. "Let her prove it."

Using my own words against me, huh? Low blow, Delphine. Low blow. I might have thought of a way out of this ambush if the headache didn't feel like it was drilling into the side of my skull. I went to the kitchen cabinet where we kept the vitamins and the pain reliever, but the medicine was missing.

"I moved the ibuprofen to the cabinet in the bathroom, where it belongs," my sister hollered, knowing as she so often did exactly what I was thinking without me saying a word.

"Thank you." I closed the cupboard door.

"While you're at it, take your blood pressure pill too. You forgot it this morning."

She was right. In my rush to get out of the house, I had missed it. I poured a glass of water, went to the powder room, and pulled a little white pill from my pillbox. Then, I fished a brown pill from the bottle of ibuprofen and took that too.

The headache was getting worse by the minute. Before I headed to the shop, maybe it would be better to lie down for a bit.

"I'm going to take a nap," I called to Del and half-expected an argument.

"All right. I hope you'll feel better once the medicine kicks in." There might have been a hint of disappointment in her voice, but she didn't stop me. I took that as a win.

As I stepped into my room, I discovered I wasn't alone. "Nap time for you too?"

Kheppy had curled into a ball in the middle of my bed. Her eyes were closed, but her ears twitched. I knew she was listening.

"Well, scoot over." I nudged her gently toward the edge of my queen-size mattress, which she tolerated without a fuss.

At some point I fell asleep because the next thing I knew, my eyes were fluttering open, and the deep slant of sunshine across the floor told me I had been out for a while.

I jumped up and instantly regretted it. I sat back down to wait for the lightheadedness to pass and noticed Kheppy hadn't moved.

She must have felt my gaze on her because she slowly stretched and opened her eyes. "Up so soon? We should sleep a little more."

"You can sleep, but I need to get to the shop. I can't sleep all day." I checked my appearance in the mirror over my dresser and pulled a hairbrush through my blue waves, while scrutinizing the thin band of gray roots already appearing in my part. "Good enough," I mumbled at my reflection. At least the headache was gone.

When I emerged from my room, I was about to scold Delphine for letting me oversleep, until I saw she had company.

A quick scan of the room confirmed what I'd suspected. She hadn't let me off the hook at all. She'd called in reinforcements.

"Seriously, Delphine? I don't have time for this. Sissy has been at the shop by herself all day. I need to get down there."

Delphine was sitting with Jemma and Opal at the dinette table, but Willa was the one who answered me. She swiveled around in our recliner and gave me one of those serious, motherly looks.

"Sissy is doing fine. Jemma checked on her a little while ago, and the girl has the shop under control. She said to tell you the discounts are working. By noon, you'd already had the best sales day of the quarter. Isn't that right, Jemma?"

"Exactly right," Jemma piped up. "Whatever you're paying her, it isn't enough."

That was probably true, but it was an issue for another day.

"Don't you have your own shop to run, Jemma? Why are you here?"

Delphine pushed back her chair and stood up. "We're all here because you need us, Boo, whether or not you want to admit it. You're trying to do what you always do and fix everything for everyone all by yourself."

"Not true," I grumbled back.

She threw up both hands. "Who wanted to drive out to see Wyatt Landon all by herself? What do you think would have happened if I hadn't insisted on going with you or the police hadn't been there? Do you think Wyatt would have calmly and rationally agreed to protect our community after you accused him of murder? What if you're wrong? Or worse, what if you're right? What would stop that alpha wolf from attacking you, Boo?"

Opal jumped up from her chair and put a consoling arm around Delphine's shoulder. "Don't work yourself up, dear. We're here. We'll figure this out."

"You four can sit here and figure it out to your hearts' content. I'm going to work." I grabbed my purse from the side table and headed for the door.

"Lucille Marie Boudreaux, you stop right there."

It was Willa's voice, but for a second, I hoped it was Kheppy playing games again. When I turned to face my old friend, her iron stare told me this was no game.

"Sissy can manage," Willa continued. "She can handle the store without you. We need you here. We came to help because this isn't just about you. This affects all of us, every single person in the supernatural community. So, you are going to accept our help. Do you understand me?"

"Yes, ma'am." Suddenly, I was a chastened schoolgirl again, standing in the principal's office.

"Good. We're due for a protection ritual anyway, so let's beef it up and see if we can shed any light on the situation." She checked her watch. "We've got a couple of hours until sundown. I say we order pizza then get to work."

By the time we finished two pizzas—mushroom without cheese for the vegans, pepperoni for the traditionalists, and a slice of each for me—we knew what we had to do.

I was in charge of gathering the lavender from the garden. Delphine harvested the laurel, and Jemma cut the rosemary. Willa and Opal assembled the candles, bowls, and chimes.

As the sky slipped into twilight, we took everything to the small clearing behind the greenhouse and formed our circle. Willa recited the usual incantation, with an added request for clarity and guidance, and then we each offered our herb bundles to the fire smoldering in the cast-iron pot at the center.

We all watched the gray smoke rise and inhaled the strong, fragrant aroma.

"Is anyone seeing anything?" Jemma asked, breaking the silence. She shot a sharp look at Opal, who tried to shush her.

Willa sighed and shook her head. "No, Jemma's right. Maybe it was too much rosemary."

"How can it be too much rosemary?" Opal said. "You can never have too much rosemary."

"Should we try again?" Jemma asked.

"We've lost the light." Willa glanced up at the darkened sky. "It'll have to wait until tomorrow."

"Not necessarily," Delphine suggested. I didn't even have to see that impish grin to know what she was thinking. "Let's go inside. It's getting chilly out here."

She rubbed her bare arms like the temperature had plummeted to zero instead of dipping a hair below sixty, according to our outdoor thermometer. Still, we all followed her inside.

I headed for the kitchen to fill the kettle, put it on the stove, and tried to think of a diplomatic way out of what I knew was coming next. "Who wants tea?"

A chorus of yeses followed, so I pulled the tea, the pot, and five cups down from the shelf.

Opal entered the kitchen and shooed me into the front room. "You don't have to wait on us. Go have a seat."

It was a sweet gesture, and if I didn't know her so well, I might have thought that was all it was. "You know what she's doing, don't you?"

That coy smile said it all.

I shook my head and handed her the box of my favorite British black tea, then joined the others.

As I'd suspected, Delphine sat at the table with her tarot deck in front of her, face down. Willa and Jemma sat alongside my sister, leaving the seat in front of the cards ready and waiting for me.

A cold knot settled in my gut. "I'd rather not do this now." Or later. Or ever.

"Let's forget about your dry spell for a minute and just give it a try." My sister smiled so sweetly, but I could see the glint of determination in her eyes. She wouldn't let this go until I obliged.

To her credit, she thought she was helping. As far as she knew, I was only avoiding the cards because they'd stopped speaking to me. It was a misconception, but one I was happy to indulge because it was easier than admitting the truth.

How could I tell her the cards hadn't stopped speaking to me? It was that I no longer wanted to listen. They had betrayed me. They'd almost ruined me.

Every muscle in my body tensed. All I wanted to do was turn around and walk out of this room. Away from that deck. Away from my sister. Away from the sweet and caring friends who thought they were being supportive.

They weren't.

"Let's just see what happens," Delphine added.

And give the cards another chance to betray me? No, thank you.

I tried to refuse, but my sister cut me off. "One card, Boo. That's all I'm asking."

If I said no, I'd have to explain myself, and not just to Delphine. I would have to admit it to all of them. I'd have to tell them about that stupid reading I did for Mallory Haines all those years ago and what had happened after. I'd have to think about it again, and I didn't want to do that. It was ancient history. I'd moved on. She'd moved on. For all I knew, she didn't even remember it.

A little voice inside whispered, *If we've all moved on, just pull the stupid card.*

"Fine. One card," I said and sat down.

Delphine pushed the deck toward me. "Cut, please."

"I know the drill." I split the deck into three piles, re-assembled them in a different order, then pushed the stack back to Delphine.

She turned the top card and placed it to the side.

Eight of Wands.

My sister's eyebrows shot up. "Swift action. Opportunities. Forward momentum. A promising card."

"If you say so," I said. "It could mean anything, though."

"Fair enough." She picked another card.

I held out my hand to stop her before she turned it over. "You said one card."

Delphine's eyes widened. "I thought you wanted clarification. And besides, *I'm* turning this one." She set the card down, face up.

Queen of Wands.

Well, that did clarify things. I pulled back my hand.

Delphine stared at the image of the woman sitting on a throne and tapped her lower lip. "An independent woman. Determined. Who do you suppose that could be?" She glanced at Jemma and Willa, who had left her chair to stand at the edge of the table.

Del's lip twitched. I knew she assumed the card represented me. They all did. "And all those wands too." My sister tapped both cards. "Interesting."

"Fascinating." I rolled my eyes, but even I had to admit, Delphine might be onto something.

When she turned a third card, I was sure of it.

Justice.

I stared at that regal figure holding a sword in one hand and golden scales in the other.

No one uttered a word. They didn't have to because the meaning was clear.

"What did I miss?" Opal asked as she arrived at the table with the tea tray. When no one answered, she looked down at the cards. "Oh. What do you think it means?"

She looked at me. They all looked at me.

"It means I have to go see Wyatt tomorrow."

Chapter 12

Impeccable Character

My PLAN TO ARRIVE at the Laguna Bay police station at seven-thirty a.m. to sneak in a visit with Wyatt Landon before Detective Platt started his day completely backfired.

The lobby was empty when I arrived, and when I flagged down a uniformed officer on the other side of the counter's thick acrylic window, he told me I'd have to wait until the clerk began his shift at the top of the hour.

So, I waited, in full view of a dozen desks crammed together in the most chaotic configuration I'd ever seen.

Of course, Detective Platt was one of those people, and he spotted me immediately, despite my efforts to blend into the lobby decor. My electric blue hair did not exactly help the situation.

"Good morning, Boo. I didn't expect you'd actually show up," he said when he approached the counter, looking smug, like he knew I'd been trying to hide from him.

"What can I say? I couldn't resist your charms." Would he notice the sarcasm? "Don't you ever go home?"

At least he'd removed his trench coat. He was wearing a starched white dress shirt with sleeves rolled to the elbows and a pair of pressed, olive-colored khakis.

Who ironed khakis, for pity's sake?

"Sometimes. When they run out of coffee." He glanced at the middle-aged man who had come up next to him. The clerk, I assumed. The detective gestured at me. "She's here to see Mr. Landon. I can walk her back."

The clerk grabbed a clipboard and ran his finger down the top sheet. "You don't have to do that, detective. I can call up a guard."

"No," Detective Platt said. "The lady and I have unfinished business anyway."

"We do?"

"Just a few questions, if you don't mind."

He wasn't fooling anybody. It didn't matter if I minded or not, even if the rebel in me was begging to say, "As a matter of fact, I do mind."

I couldn't imagine a scenario where that would work in my favor, so I kept my mouth shut and followed him when he led me behind the counter and back through the sea of desks and putty-colored cubicles.

We stopped at a metal desk at the far end of the room. It was bare except for a computer and a phone. No photos or mementos. No files or pen-filled mugs. Not even a nameplate.

"Have a seat," he said, tapping the backrest of the adjacent metal chair before dropping into the desk chair and pulling a skinny notepad from his shirt pocket.

I sat. "When can I see Wyatt?"

"You said you've known Mr. Landon for quite some time. Were you aware he had a relationship with the victim, Ms. Blake?"

I debated whether to repeat my question but decided against it. This was his turf, and being obstinate might feel satisfying for a moment, but ultimately, it wouldn't help me.

"I was, but not until yesterday."

His head popped up from his notepad. "What happened yesterday?"

"Look, you said I could speak to Wyatt. Are you going back on your word?"

"You didn't answer my question."

True, but something told me I shouldn't. I returned his icy stare. "You don't like me, do you, Detective?"

He leaned back in his chair. "On the contrary. You remind me of my grandmother."

"Oh? She must be a charming woman."

Was he sucking in his cheeks to stifle a grin? "Absolutely," he said, "and once she puts her mind to something, there's no stopping her."

"You're right," I said. "We are alike." Maybe this guy was smarter than he looked. "So, when are you going to let me talk to Wyatt?"

He chuckled softly and wrote something in his notepad. "All right, but after you talk to him, we need to finish our conversation."

Score one for me. "Sure, Detective. It's a date."

A night in jail had taken its toll on Wyatt Landon. When the man entered the room wearing an orange jumpsuit with a uniformed officer at his elbow, the gaze that had burned with blue fire the day before now stared blankly at the floor. The limbs that had been tense and rigid drooped like overcooked noodles. Somehow, even that sharp-edged jaw had gone soft.

Is that what guilt did to a man?

Is that what it did to a wolf?

The officer nudged Wyatt toward the metal table where I was waiting. He didn't look at me until he'd settled into the chair.

"Did you come to bail me out?" He leaned back and stared at me.

"May we have some privacy?" I asked the guard as he closed the door but remained in the room.

"I can't leave, ma'am." The young man stood at attention with his hands clasped in front.

How were Wyatt and I supposed to have a frank discussion with a normie in the room?

"That can't be true. I see people having private conversations in the crime shows all the time."

"This isn't television, ma'am. Unless it involves a lawyer, visits are supervised." That rock-solid gaze never left the opposite wall.

"But I'm his lawyer."

He didn't believe me. His smirk said as much. And why should he? I was lying through my teeth.

Yet desperate times called for desperate measures.

"Go ask the detective," I added, doubling down on my deception. "He'll tell you. I'm part of a senior emeritus outreach program through the community college."

Apparently, I could lie up a storm once I got going.

The guard turned to me, and I held his gaze. If he sensed weakness, it was over.

"Fine," he said, then turned and grabbed the doorknob.

"No cameras, right? Or microphones?" I had to be clear on that point. Everything depended on it.

He looked back over his shoulder. "No cameras or microphones. Nobody will be listening. Knock on the door when you're ready to leave."

When the officer left and the door's lock latched, Wyatt chuckled. "I didn't know you were a lawyer, Boo."

"I'm not. But hopefully he won't figure that out until after we've finished our chat."

I folded my hands on the tabletop, stared at the man who might have killed Isabelle Blake, and tried not to let my fear distract me from what needed to be done. "I'm sure you had your reasons for doing what you did to Isabelle," I said. "But you can't take everyone down with you. Think of your family, your pack, if nothing else."

Wyatt leaned forward and fixed me with a predator's gaze that made me wonder if the guard was close enough to hear me scream.

"I did nothing to Isabelle," he growled. "I don't even know why I'm in this place. They told me she was found in your shop. Maybe you're the one who should be wearing a jumpsuit."

If he were trying to intimidate me, it was working. I swallowed hard. "Maybe it's because they know about the baby."

His angry red face turned white as a sheet. "How do you know about that?"

"Deductive reasoning." And Willa's razor-sharp eyes. There was no reason to bring her into this, though. "Tell me, was Isabelle like you?" It was a theory I'd been considering since learning about the two of them.

"If you mean"—he stopped and glanced at the closed door, then lowered his voice another octave—"if you mean a wolf, then no. And before you ask your next question, no, I didn't tell her that's what I was, either." His gaze dropped. "I was going through some things back then. I didn't like what I was, and foolishly, I thought I could wish it away. Being with her was part of my trying to do that."

His voice seemed to catch in his throat with those last few words. He rubbed his face with both palms as if he were rubbing away the emotion.

It wasn't the reaction I'd expected. Either Wyatt really was innocent, or he was one heck of an actor.

"Look," he said, pulling his hands away from his now-bloodshot eyes. "When it happened, I was young. We were both young, and I wanted to do the right thing. I asked her to marry me, but she left. Like, *poof!* One day she was just gone, and I never heard from her again."

"Didn't you try to find her?"

He leaned on one elbow and closed his eyes. "Not really. I'd told her how I felt, but I figured it was her decision. And it wasn't like I was in any position to care for a baby. Not then."

"I had no idea about any of this, Wyatt. I'm so sorry." That wasn't a lie. I *was* sorry. It broke my heart to think how painful that situation must have been for those two young people. "Considering everything, it would understandably have made you angry. It would have made anyone angry."

He shook his head. "You're thinking I was angry enough to kill her, but you're wrong. I didn't even know she was back. Not for certain, anyway. I thought I caught a whiff of her scent off my son when he went into town last week, but I didn't want to believe it. I certainly didn't go into town myself to confirm it."

Was that true? The way he looked at me, the conviction in his voice, it seemed to be. But I couldn't shake the thought that the pain she must have caused him was so deep and so profound, how could he ever have forgiven her?

"You still think I did it, don't you?"

His animal instinct was right on target.

When I said nothing, his head dropped back. He stared at the ceiling. "Maybe the girl found out her mother came back. Did you ever think of that?"

"The girl? Is your daughter still here? I thought you didn't know what happened after Isabelle left."

"Some psychic you are," he muttered.

"I never said I was psychic. I'm a card reader." Who no longer read cards, but that technicality was hardly worth mentioning. Like the fact Khepeset wasn't my familiar, as most of our friends believed. Technically, I was hers.

"Fine. Whatever." He flipped his hand dismissively. "I didn't know what happened to Isabelle. But she contacted me after she gave birth to tell me she was giving our baby up for adoption. She was going to do it on her own, but I told her I wanted to help. Which I did. So, to answer your question, yes. The girl is here. Right under your nose, in fact. It's Sissy Meyers."

Chapter 13

The Interview

"Your daughter is my shop clerk?" I don't know how I got the question out because my jaw felt like a stone scraping across the linoleum. How was sweet Sissy related to this brute? And how could she keep that from me?

Unless she didn't know. She'd never once mentioned being adopted. "Does Sissy know? Does she know what she is?"

He shook his head.

"How could you keep it from her? What if she transforms? Do her parents know?" The questions tumbled out, one after another. Each more troubling than the last.

"Her mother does. She's a super too. Sort of."

"What do you mean, *sort of*?" Being a super was like being pregnant. You were, or you weren't. There wasn't an in-between.

"Sissy's mom, Beth, comes from a line of werepanthers who settled here about the same time my parents did. Our parents socialized occasionally, so I knew about her situation."

I vaguely remembered a group of werepanthers settling in the canyon, but they left years ago. At least I thought they had.

"What was her situation?"

He shifted in his seat. "This is private. Okay? It can't leave this room."

This was getting worse by the minute. What had they done to poor Sissy?

"Of course," I said, but all I was thinking was, *If you put Sissy in danger, I will end you.*

"Beth's family came here looking for help because Beth couldn't transform. Ever. They tried everything, but she was essentially human. She was only twelve when they abandoned her, and she's been living as a normie ever since."

"That's horrible. How could they leave their child?"

"My parents helped them find a good family. They thought they were doing the best thing for her since they couldn't change who—or what—they were. Anyway, when Isabelle called me about the pregnancy, I knew Beth and her husband—a total normie who knew nothing of her past—were struggling to conceive. When I suggested the adoption to Beth, she jumped at the chance. She said it was an answer to their prayers."

"But what about Sissy? She's half werewolf. Does she even know?"

Wyatt shook his head. "I never said anything to Isabelle. Honestly, I was afraid to. I didn't know if our daughter was human or werewolf, but Beth and I talked about it.

We both looked for signs, but Sissy has never shown any. Beth remembers a lot from her time with her werepanther family. She knows what to look for. I also told her I'd step in if anything ever happened with Sissy."

"So, you arranged the adoption," I said, still trying to wrap my mind around what he'd told me. "Which kept Sissy close enough for you to keep tabs on her."

He shrugged. "Basically."

"And she's never changed? You're sure?"

"It's a recessive gene. She carries it, but it hasn't manifested."

"Is it possible Isabelle told Sissy about any of this?"

He threw up his hands. "I suppose anything is possible. All I know is Isabelle never came to see me. If she was in your shop, she was probably there to see Sissy."

I didn't want to admit it, but that seemed possible. Maybe even probable. I chewed my lip as I tried to think back to that morning. Sissy had left at the same time I did. She wasn't in the shop.

But what did it matter? This was Sissy we were talking about. Kind, sweet Sissy, who wouldn't hurt anyone, let alone her own mother.

"Can you think of any other explanation?" There had to be something—anything—that would make sense of this.

He shook his head. I racked my brain, but all I came up with was the uncomfortable sense that, while I couldn't imagine Sissy harming Isabelle, I also no longer believed Wyatt had either.

The doorknob turned, and before I knew it, Detective Platt was standing in the interrogation room, glaring at me. "What's this nonsense about you being Mr. Landon's lawyer?"

Busted. Wyatt looked at me, offering no help at all.

"Who said I was Mr. Landon's lawyer?" I asked.

"That's what you told the guard." The detective turned, and standing behind him was that officer, sneering at me.

"That's right, Detective. That's what she told me."

How was I going to get out of this? Then it struck me. Play the old-lady card. As much as I hated to do it, I had no choice.

I chuckled and shook my head. "Oh goodness, you'll have to excuse me. I might have mixed it up. Sometimes I get so confused. What I meant to say, young man, was I'm here as an advocate for Mr. Landon. I'm allowed to do that, aren't I?"

Detective Platt motioned the guard toward Wyatt. "Take him back to his cell. This visit is over."

"With pleasure." The guard brushed past the detective to grab Wyatt's arm.

Before he made contact and before I knew what was happening, Wyatt lunged across the table, grabbed my wrist, and yanked me toward him. The movement was too sudden for me to resist, and instantly, the guard and the detective pulled their weapons and aimed them squarely at Wyatt.

"Release her, Landon!" the detective yelled.

Fear froze a scream in my throat as Wyatt pushed his head toward mine. My eyes squeezed shut, terrified of what he would do next. Bite me? Kill me?

It was neither. He whispered hoarsely. "Get me out before the full moon. If I change here, I'm done for."

Then he released me, and when I opened my eyes, Wyatt was kneeling on the floor, his fingers laced behind his head.

"Get her out of here." The detective waved at the guard, who pulled me toward the door.

"Please don't hurt him," I wailed, too panicked to compose myself as the guard pushed me into the hallway. "He didn't hurt me. He was never going to hurt me."

I wasn't sure if that was entirely true, or if my pleas made any difference, but I had to try, for Wyatt's sake. I was already pretty sure he wasn't the killer, but the desperation in his voice convinced me beyond any doubt. He was terrified, and now I was too.

If he was still in his cell when the full moon hit, he was right—he'd be done for. And if the police discovered a werewolf had been living in Laguna Bay all this time, they might uncover the truth about the rest of us too.

Chapter 14

Lemon Curd Comfort

I STOOD AT THE edge of the garden, where Delphine was on her knees, carrying out a search-and-destroy mission for weeds among the chamomile blooms.

She tossed an offender into the bucket beside her, rolled back on her heels, and adjusted the straw hat protecting her face from the midmorning sun. "You don't really believe Sissy could do such a thing, do you? She's such a darling girl."

"Under the right conditions, anyone might be capable of murder." It pained me to say it, but someone had killed Isabelle Blake. It wasn't me, and I doubted it was Wyatt. Sissy, unfortunately, had a motive.

When Wyatt had laid out his story, I wanted to dismiss his implication that Sissy could be the killer as a desperate attempt to throw suspicion off of himself. After leaving the police station—which I did with strict orders from Detective Platt not to return unless I wanted to end up in a jail cell of my own—I tried to convince myself it was impossible. That Sissy couldn't kill anyone.

But I kept coming back to the notion that, if Isabelle had ambushed Sissy with horrible revelations about her past, maybe Sissy had snapped.

I'd planned to go straight from the station to the shop. With Halloween only a day away, sales were more important than ever. Still, the idea of seeing Sissy made me falter.

What would I say to her? What *could* I say? I kept replaying that moment when I left the shop to collect the cupcakes from Delphine and Sissy had returned to the hardware store. I hadn't actually seen her leave.

Later, as we stood on the sidewalk while the police taped off the crime scene, she'd told me she'd left right away, but had she? I'd always despised the Big Brother surveillance cameras used in some shops, but I had to admit, one of those systems would have helped me confirm her story.

That's when I knew I needed a reality check before I went anywhere near Sissy. Spying on that girl wasn't the answer. What I needed was an unbiased perspective.

I sipped the green tea I'd taken with me to the garden. A freshly brewed pot, I hoped, would calm my frazzled nerves. But even with the tea and an attentive Kheppy brushing against my ankles, I was still on edge.

"What else did Wyatt say?" Delphine asked, wiping a bead of perspiration off her brow with the back of her sturdy, floral-print gloves.

"You mean, besides Sissy being his daughter and her having a motive for murder?" It sounded so ridiculous when I said it aloud, and not at all like the earth-shattering revelation that had hounded me all the way home. "Only that I had to help him get out of jail before the full moon."

She tossed another weed into the bucket and glanced at me. "You said he was innocent. Why are the police still holding him if he's innocent?"

"They won't exactly take my word for it," I said.

She pulled off her gloves. "No, I suppose they wouldn't. But if we can't get him out, that's going to be a problem. A big problem."

"I agree, but what can I do about it?" When I scooped up Kheppy, who had curled up for a nap in the dry bird-bath, and followed my sister toward the house, the cat yowled at me.

"Excuse me, but we've got bigger problems than your beauty rest." I set her on the porch, beside her water bowl. "But if you have a solution to our looming werewolf emergency, you go right ahead and let me know."

Kheppy rarely understood sarcasm, so I wasn't surprised when she followed me through the door, hopped up on the kitchen counter, and gave me a puzzled look. "How should I know what to do about a werewolf? I don't like them, and I don't understand them. Perhaps you should ask someone who does."

Delphine was pouring herself a cup of tea from the pot. "She has a point. You shouldn't be carrying this burden alone, and Kheppy and I can't offer much help. You need to speak to his people."

She meant his pack.

I dropped into a chair at the dinette table. "You're right. That's what I should do."

Kheppy watched me. "That's what you *should* do," she repeated. "But it's not what you *will* do, is it?"

"You are correct," Delphine said, with a note of exaggerated exasperation.

Sometimes, when you've lived with another creature for your entire life, they know you better than you know yourself. I had two such creatures. Both of them seemed to be waiting for me to catch up to the conclusion they had already reached.

It didn't make it any easier for me. I knew what they wanted me to say and what they expected me to say, but I was still mentally working through my options.

"I'm hungry," I said, because I was, and I also wanted to buy some time. "Anyone else interested in a tuna sandwich?"

Kheppy's enthusiastic "I am!" was no surprise.

As I got up to pull a pouch of tuna from the pantry and the other ingredients from the refrigerator, my sister grabbed the bread from the other end of the counter and handed it to me. She also pulled a yellow pastry box out of a bag I hadn't noticed on the table and set it down in front of me.

"I meant to tell you Luna came by after you left for the police station. She apologized again for not making it to the last Sunday dinner and dropped off a dozen of your favorite lemon curd cupcakes to make up for it."

"She didn't have to do that." My granddaughter had been coming to our Sunday dinners nearly every week since she moved to Citrus Grove. It wasn't far, but her new bakery was keeping her so busy, we were seeing less and less of her lately.

A dozen of her lemon curd cupcakes would never replace her sparkling smile or her warm hugs, but they were a delicious consolation prize.

I opened the box and gazed at the frosted beauties. "She should have told me she was coming. I hated missing her. You didn't tell her about..."

My sister shook her head. "Luna has enough going on. I didn't want to worry her."

"That's for the best." I picked a cupcake and bit into it. The tangy sweetness was pure perfection.

"I do not like cupcakes," Kheppy announced from where she was still sitting on the table. "You promised tuna."

It hadn't technically been a promise, but I'd never win that argument. "Yes, Kheppy. I will get your tuna." Not before I took another heavenly bite, though.

As I added the tuna to a bowl along with a dollop of mayonnaise and a little chopped dill pickle, Delphine continued to hover over me in the kitchen. She was nearly as impatient as the cat, just not for food.

"You already know what I'm going to say, so why do I have to say it?" I blended the tuna mixture with a fork.

"I would still like to hear it," she said.

"Fine. I don't think we should ask Wyatt's pack for help. They're all hotheads, and they would probably want to do something drastic that would make things worse." I cast a sideways glance to catch her expression.

She was nodding. Good. It gave me the courage to continue. "What we need is a Midnight Council meeting."

I expected her to balk. We hadn't had a gathering of the supernatural community in years because it could be dangerous to have so many of us in the same place at the same time. Not only did we risk being discovered by normies, but not everyone in our community played well with others. Grudges tended to linger for decades, or longer, especially among the oldest members.

My sister said nothing. Even Kheppy remained quiet. Both of them stared back at me with such blank expressions, I had no idea what they were thinking.

"Do you think it's a mistake?" I asked.

"No," she said. "It could be dangerous, but it's not fair to keep the others in the dark. I'll start the message tree."

Then she gave me one of those long, sisterly looks.

I nodded. She didn't have to tell me. I knew what I had to do.

Chapter 15

Better with Tea

WHILE DELPHINE MADE CALLS to convene the Midnight Council, the town hall-style meeting for our supernatural community, I headed over to the shop. I wanted to check on sales, but I also needed to see for myself if what Wyatt had told me about Sissy was true.

To do that, I had to speak with her face-to-face. Before my interview with Wyatt, I'd assumed my shop clerk knew as little about Isabelle Blake as I did. But could she have been hiding the truth?

My plan was to ask her point-blank if she knew the woman, then watch her eyes when she answered. I knew Sissy well enough to spot deception in her expression, if I were looking for it.

I left the house dead set on confronting the girl. But the closer I got to the shop, the more my conviction faltered. Was I giving myself too much credit? If she had already lied to me without raising any red flags, who was to say she couldn't do it again?

Was I even capable of spotting the truth? No matter how much I wanted to believe I was a rational, reasonable person, I knew in my heart I wanted Sissy to be innocent. I liked her.

Maybe I couldn't trust myself.

Which meant I might need a different approach.

Luckily, I had another idea.

A few minutes later, I pulled up to a white bungalow perched on a hillside with a distant view of the Pacific Ocean. The family's old hatchback sat in the driveway—the same one Beth Meyers had been using to ferry Sissy to the shop since the girl had given up her e-bike. Beth was home.

As I sat behind the wheel, struggling to muster the nerve to knock on the door, Sissy's mother came around the side of her house with the hose. She was watering the hydrangea bushes with their pink blooms that lined the eastern wall. When she turned the hose on the lavender bushes along the white picket fence, she spotted me and waved.

No turning back now.

I stepped to the curb with a smile to hide my sudden urge to race back down the hill to avoid this conversation. What do they say about pulling up your big-girl panties?

"Boo, hello!" She waved the water spray over the lawn. "I almost didn't recognize you. Sissy told me you'd dyed your hair. I have to say, that blue suits you. You sure know how to keep things interesting."

I brushed back the azure strands that had fallen over my shoulder. "I figure when you're as old as I am, it's best to keep people guessing."

She chuckled, but then the creases on her forehead deepened. "Is there a problem at the shop? I dropped Sissy off earlier than usual. Is she all right?"

Considering someone had died there two days ago, her concern was understandable.

"Everything is fine." At least for the moment. "Do you have a minute? There's something I'd like to ask you."

As she twisted the nozzle to stop the water flow, I could tell I hadn't completely eased her mind. "Of course. Would you like to come inside? I'll fix some tea. A friendly chat is always better with tea. My mother used to say that."

"I would love a cup. Thank you." I smiled and did my best to remember my manners. It wouldn't help anyone if I just blurted my suspicions here on the street.

I followed her into the house after she coiled the hose and stashed it near the porch.

"I haven't seen you in a while," I said. "How have you been?"

I didn't know Beth well, but the two of us used to talk in the mornings when Sissy first started at the shop. Beth would drop her off and stick around for a bit.

That had stopped when Sissy started riding an e-bike. That lasted until a few weeks ago. Now, she was back to relying on her mom. Beth hadn't resumed her morning visits, though.

Maybe she was busy, or maybe it was something else.

"I'm good, thank you," she said. "I started an herb garden in the back. Just cilantro, basil, and some chives to start. If they do well, I'd like to add other things. Opal has been a big help. I was actually thinking about joining the Laguna Bay Horticultural Society."

I did my best to maintain a casual smile, so she wouldn't notice my sudden panic.

"Opal mentioned you're both members, and that was how you knew each other," she said as she filled the kettle at the faucet and placed it on the stove.

"That's right." How much did Opal know about her neighbor, I wondered? Was she aware of Beth's past or heritage? Or Sissy's?

I hadn't considered that possibility, and now it had my brain working overtime.

"It sounds like the kind of thing I've been looking for. You know, something to get me out of the house once in a while. I couldn't find any information about the meetings, though," she said. "Did I get the name wrong?"

That was the problem with a name like Laguna Bay Horticultural Society. People thought we were an ordinary gardening club, even though we never advertised or held any public meetings, events, or activities. And new members were considered on a strict, invitation-only basis.

I raised the issue a couple of times to the group, but Willa rightfully pointed out that calling ourselves something like the Laguna Bay Psychic Readers and Kitchen Witches, which might be more accurate, would probably scare the normies.

Still, I made a mental note to address the matter again at our next meeting.

"You have the right name, but we're going through some changes," I said. "That's a good point about the website, though. We'll have to consider that."

We wouldn't of course, but I was trying to keep the conversation positive.

As she prepared the teapot and the cups, I got to the reason for my visit.

"Does Sissy know Isabelle Blake was her birth mother?" The question had sounded so much better in my head, but it was too late to reel it back in.

Beth had her back to me as she spooned loose-leaf tea into her pretty botanical-print pot, but I watched her shoulders slump with the weight of the question.

It took a full minute for her to answer. "How do you know about that?"

If I wanted her honesty, I figured I owed it to her to be honest too. "Wyatt told me."

She tensed again. "Did he say anything else?"

She wanted to know if he'd told me about her past and probably her connection to the supernatural community.

"Nothing worth mentioning," I said in a way that I hoped would make her understand her lineage was not my concern. In fact, under different circumstances, I would be reassuring her that her secret was safe with me, and that there was a whole community of us who would welcome her, if she ever chose to reveal herself. Someday, I hoped we could have that conversation. Today, however, I needed to focus on Sissy.

Beth's continued silence told me she needed time to absorb the fact that I knew her secret, so I stopped talking and gave her space.

She busied herself with getting the teapot and cups onto a tray and adding a sugar bowl and a couple of teaspoons. When she turned around, it was as if a dark cloud had settled over her. She walked the tray to the breakfast nook and gestured for me to sit, which I did without a word.

When we were settled and the peaches-and-cream aroma wafted from the flavored black tea, she said, "The short answer is no. I didn't tell Sissy about Isabelle."

I stared at the tendrils of steam rising from my cup.

"She doesn't even know about Wyatt, although she has met him," Beth continued. "In the early years, he told me he would always come if we needed him, but he preferred to stay away. It was too painful, he said. I respected that."

As a mother separated from her own child for too many years to count, I didn't understand it, but Wyatt's situation was different.

"After his wedding," she continued, "and having another child, he changed. He came around more often."

"Was that awkward for you?"

She shook her head, but a twitch at the corner of her mouth told another story.

"He had every right to see Sissy." She picked up her teacup and held it near her lips without sipping, as if it were a shield.

"Did he ever take her to Landon Fields?" I pressed. "Or introduce her to the rest of his family?"

She lowered the cup slightly. "No. I asked him not to do that. It's always been an understanding between us that she may be his blood, but she was my daughter. I've heard stories about how competitive his family can be, and I didn't want to subject my sweet baby girl to that. She knows nothing about the community."

It was clear she meant the supernatural community.

She also raised an interesting point. Wyatt's son must have assumed he was his father's heir. What would happen if he discovered Sissy was the true firstborn?

Wyatt was still a strong and virile man, but eventually his health would decline, and an heir would have to take over the business and the pack. If that notion had occurred to me, it must have occurred to his son.

It was an interesting quagmire, but I couldn't see how it had any bearing on Isabelle's murder. What I was slowly realizing, however, was how deftly Beth had shifted the conversation toward Wyatt.

"Did you know Isabelle Blake had come back to town?" I asked.

She hid her lips behind her teacup again.

I waited, resisting the urge to fill the awkward silence.

Finally, Beth sipped and lowered the cup. "No, I didn't. Not until Sissy told me what happened at the shop two days ago. Such a tragedy. Sissy says the police have been awful. How could they suspect you, of all people?"

Oh boy, she was good. Deflect, deflect, deflect. "The boys in blue were only doing their job. No harm was done."

"Right. And now they have their man. Poor Wyatt. I can only imagine the pain that woman put him through to push him to such an extreme measure."

"You believe he's guilty?"

She straightened, and some of the brightness returned to her expression. "Well, sure. We all know what were-wolves are capable of when they're angry. I mean, it's not exactly a surprise."

I swallowed hard. "No, I suppose it isn't."

What was a surprise was how easily this woman turned on a man who considered her a friend. Sure, Wyatt had his anger issues, but he'd also given her the greatest gift she'd ever received in her life: her daughter.

Then again, he had not-so-subtly pointed a finger at Sissy.

As Beth downed the rest of her tea, I struggled with mine because I had learned nothing that exonerated Sissy. And there were plenty of reasons to think Beth Meyers might be just as capable of the crime.

Chapter 16

Bloody Knuckles

SISSY WAS HELPING A customer in the mask section when I walked in, but she pulled away as soon as she saw me.

"Before you go back to the office, I have to explain something. It's about the candy." When she slid between me and the hallway to the back rooms, she was biting her bottom lip. Never a good sign.

"Is there a problem?" Was she going to tell me the candy wouldn't arrive in time? Was I going to have to make an emergency trip to the wholesale store so we wouldn't disappoint the trick-or-treaters?

"Well…" She stretched the word into five syllables.

"Well?" I snapped back.

"The candy arrived."

That should be good news, but her pained expression told me it wasn't.

"And?" I was really trying not to lose my patience.

"And I made a little mistake."

"How little?"

"I must have misread the listing."

"We got the wrong candy?" Was I about to be the lame shop handing out hard candy?

Her clasped fingers twisted and squeezed. "It's the right candy. We just got a lot more of it than we needed. Instead of twenty boxes of individually packaged gummy worms and spiders, I ordered twenty cases."

"What's the difference?"

"There are ten boxes in each case."

I quickly did the math. "We have two hundred boxes of candy?"

She winced and nodded at the same time. "But I think it might be a good thing."

"Why? Can we return some of it?"

Her hopeful smile tipped into a frown. "No, but look. I completely filled the cauldron, so it's not empty anymore."

I went back to the front of the shop and looked at the window display. My not-so-wicked witch was standing over her cauldron, which wasn't bubbling with green slime, but it was overflowing with little cellophane packets of gummy spiders and worms.

"The kids might love grabbing their candy straight from the cauldron," she added.

I had to stand there for a moment to let that sink in, but once it had, I nodded. "That might actually work." It surprised me, but turning the cauldron into a giant candy bowl was an even better idea than the green slime.

It seemed to surprise Sissy too.

"You aren't mad?" she asked, her expression caught somewhere between fear and relief.

A wave of guilt washed over me. Here she was, panicking over a mix-up while I was secretly meeting with her mother to dig up dirt to prove Sissy might be a killer. At least I'd come away thinking Beth was the more likely suspect.

The repercussions of that realization suddenly hit me. Sissy was not only going to learn that the woman who died in that now-gummy-filled cauldron was her biological mother, if she didn't already know it, but also that the mother who had raised her was the killer.

When all that came out, would Sissy ever recover? Would she hate me for being the one to drag it into the light?

"No, Sissy," I said. "I'm not mad. Not in the least. You made it work, and I appreciate it. Thank you." Before my emotions got the better of me, I patted her on the shoulder and rushed back to the office, where I collapsed into the desk chair and dropped my head into my hands.

What if Beth told Sissy I'd visited her? I'd worried about that the entire drive back to the shop. But no, I decided. If Beth hadn't told Sissy the truth about Isabelle by now, she probably never would.

Unfortunately, that didn't make me feel better. It only added to my guilt because now I was hiding the truth from Sissy too.

And Wyatt! Yet another secret I was keeping from her. How could I ever look that young woman in the eye again?

The sound of feet scuffling on the floorboards behind me made me freeze. Those weren't kitty feet. I'd left Kheppy with Delphine, and my sister would have called if she'd planned to drop the cat off at the shop.

Someone cleared their throat.

It definitely wasn't Kheppy, and it wasn't Sissy. I could hear her in the shop with a customer, explaining the difference between the inflatable goblins and the light-projected ghouls.

I spun around to see who had dared to enter the room clearly marked with a "Staff Only" sign.

A lanky young man wearing an old T-shirt bearing the logo of a band he was far too young to appreciate stood in front of the mini fridge, sipping from a can of orange soda. My *personal supply* of imported orange soda.

"Hey, Ms. Boudreaux. Sissy said it would be okay for me to hang out back here. I'm Ryan. Remember? We met a couple of days ago."

Right. Sissy's boyfriend.

"She lets me come back here sometimes when she's in the shop alone. You know, like a bodyguard." He took a long gulp from the can.

"Of course. I see you found our fridge."

He held out the can and looked at it. "Yeah. I love this brand. You hardly ever see it in stores anymore. It's so cool you have it."

"It certainly is." I considered telling him I drove across town once a month because it was my favorite, but I figured the veiled message that it was supposed to be off limits would be lost on him. He seemed more interested in the white gauze wrapped around his right hand, anyway.

The gauze appeared new. Then I noticed the shop's first-aid kit at the edge of my desk. "What happened here?"

My question was drowned out by Merle's booming voice. "Boo, good. You're back."

He stepped into the doorway and touched the tip of his cowboy hat. His usual greeting. The instant I saw him, I remembered my promise to call him when I'd finished at Landon Fields. A promise I'd completely forgotten until this moment.

"What are you doing here, Merle?" Was he here to scold me for not calling? I braced.

My lack of enthusiasm didn't go unnoticed. He stepped back, but his smile widened. "What kind of greeting is that for your new handyman?"

"My new what?" This day was already weird, and it wasn't even noon.

He chuckled and entered the office, which was decently sized for one person. With two, it was cozy. Three? Not so much.

"I've almost got those pipes behind the sink in good shape. I was planning to tackle the wiring issue this afternoon."

"Oh? So, you aren't mad? I realize I forgot to call, like I said I would yesterday."

He waved away the concern. "I was at the police department when they brought Wyatt in."

"Did you hear what happened?"

"The gist of it," he said with a shrug. "Sorry it didn't go the way you'd hoped."

"Me too," I said.

He touched his hat again. "I just need to grab a few things at the hardware store, then I'll get back to the repairs. Are you ready, Ryan?"

Ryan waved him off. "I told you, Mr. Foster, I have Sissy's e-bike, so I've got a ride."

That explains what happened to the bike.

Merle wrinkled his nose. "It's no problem, son. Sissy needs her bike to get home. Otherwise, she'll need to call her mother for a ride. Besides, there's an urgent care clinic a block from Howard's place. I'll drop you off, get what I need, pick you up, and deliver you to the Beachside Café. If we leave now, we can be sure to get you there in plenty of time for your shift. What do you say?"

When Ryan still hesitated, Merle added, "I wasn't going to mention it, but you'd be doing me a favor, son. I've been thinking about signing up to be a driver on one of those rideshare things to make a few extra bucks. This would be good practice for me."

Ryan gazed up at him. "So, like, you want me to rate your service?" Was that a smirk on his face?

"Exactly. Any feedback would be appreciated."

If I hadn't seen that twinkle in Merle's eye, I wouldn't have known he was telling a whopper of a lie. Ryan, however, seemed completely fooled.

"Have you stocked water bottles and snacks in the back seat?" the young man asked. "Because that's always important if you want a good rating."

Merle rubbed his chin. "No, the thought hadn't occurred to me. You see there? You're already teaching me so much."

"If you don't have water, I'll just grab another one of these, and we can hit the road." He crumpled the orange can in his hand and tossed it in the trash bin before pulling the last one from the fridge.

I nearly stopped him, but Merle had his hand on the young man's shoulder and was firmly pushing him out the door. I figured the soda was a small price to pay if it meant my pipes and wiring might actually get fixed before the inspector returned.

As the men said their goodbyes to Sissy, who was still assisting the customer, I stood in front of the open fridge, wishing there was something in there to drink besides that old can of diet grape soda. I was considering whether I needed to make an emergency run across town when Merle rushed back into the office, alone and gasping for breath. He closed the door behind him.

Before I could ask what he was doing, his hand shot out to stop me. "That kid could be trouble," he said between gulps of air.

"Who? Ryan?"

His index finger flew to his lips. "I didn't want to say anything in front of Sissy," he whispered. "But did you notice the bandage on his hand?"

I nodded.

"When I arrived, Sissy was fixing him up. There were bloody paper towels everywhere. Those knuckles took a serious beating. Or did the beating, which is probably what actually happened."

"He hit Sissy?" It was the first thing that jumped into my head, and even though I hadn't seen any signs of battery on the girl when I walked in, I was prepared to go after that young man myself and tear him apart.

"Calm down, tiger," Merle said. "Sissy told me it was a delivery guy. He came in with some boxes. Sissy said she tried to refuse them, but the guy wouldn't take them back. Ryan took it upon himself to get involved."

"By punching him?"

"No. She said Ryan confronted the guy. Not physically but basically screamed at him as he left."

Clearly, I'd missed something. "When did they fight?"

Merle sighed. "That's the thing. Sissy said after the delivery guy left, Ryan was so worked up, he punched the door frame, like three times and full force. I wouldn't have believed someone could hurt themselves like that, but I showed up soon after and saw those bloody knuckles myself. I've never seen that much anger from a normie."

"Was Sissy upset?" I imagined the girl would have been terrified by that behavior.

"She was so calm about it. That's what worried me. You know what she said? 'He's so protective. He'd do anything for me.' Boo, it didn't faze her. It was like this was a regular thing. I tell you, that boy's temper is going to get somebody hurt."

I shared the concern. I also had to wonder if maybe it already had.

Chapter 17
Costume Shopper

AVOIDING SISSY OCCUPIED THE rest of my day. Mostly, I hid out in the shop's office and tried to be productive by catching up on emails and invoices.

Once those chores were done, I resorted to tidying the desk's top drawer, which had become a jumbled mess of leaky pens, stubby pencils, and bent paper clips, with an absurd number of plastic tape dispensers tossed in. How had I accumulated seven of them, and each one less than half used?

It was probably a miracle we had office supplies at all, considering I couldn't even remember the last time I'd bought any of that stuff.

Which meant Sissy had.

Without being asked and with no thanks, just like she'd been doing so much around the shop.

Jemma's words echoed in my ears. *Whatever you're paying her, it isn't enough.*

If I'd learned anything through this ordeal with Isabelle Blake, it was that I had been taking Sissy Meyers for granted.

It shamed me to think I'd ever thought she could be the killer. At least I'd realized my error quickly. Unfortunately, that would be little consolation to Sissy if someone she loved turned out to be the murderer, which now seemed inevitable.

In Beth Meyers's rush to throw suspicion on Wyatt, she had only made herself look more guilty. I didn't think Beth was a bad person, but even nice people could do bad things in extreme circumstances. Had she panicked when she learned her daughter's birth mother had returned? Had she tried to confront the woman, and the encounter turned ugly? It was the scenario I'd envisioned between Sissy and Isabelle, but Beth and her maternal instincts seemed far more likely.

That had been true—until I learned about Ryan's bloody knuckles. I'd never encountered a normie with such a violent temper. If he was trying to protect Sissy from a stubborn delivery man, I could only imagine what he could do to a birth mother who had abandoned her at birth.

Could he have been in the shop when Isabelle showed up? I wouldn't have thought so, but after today, I wasn't sure. He had been awfully comfortable back here on his own.

Isabelle might have entered the shop while he was here with Sissy. If Isabelle confronted Sissy or there was an argument, I could see him sending Sissy away while he dealt with Isabelle.

The more I thought about it, the more compelling that scenario seemed. Ryan was a hothead with violent tendencies. Beth grew lovely hydrangeas and lavender, served tea from a teapot, and raised a sweet, beautiful daughter.

"I'll check in the back to see if we have that item in stock."

Sissy's voice, loud enough to carry from the sales floor, interrupted my mental murder trial, partly because it seemed intentionally loud and partly because we kept no stock in the back. Ever.

When she opened the office door, I swiveled around to ask what was up. Her expression said it all.

Her cheeks had lost their usual rosy color, and her breathing was shaky.

I jumped from the chair and dropped the tangle of interlinked paper clips I was trying to separate. "What's wrong, dear?"

She took a deep breath as if to steady herself. "There's a guy out there asking about werewolf costumes. I showed him what we have, but he said they aren't right. I don't know what to tell him, and... Boo, he scares me."

My jaw tensed. "You said werewolf costumes?"

"Yeah, it's the only thing he wants. He can see what we have, so I'm not sure what he expects me to do."

Unfortunately, if the unreasonable customer was who I thought it was, I didn't think he was here for a costume at all. I grabbed my wallet from my purse, pulled out a few bills, and handed them to her.

"You've been doing a wonderful job. Why don't you take a break and treat yourself to one of those fancy coffees you like?"

She stared at the cash, stunned. "Really?"

Her surprise was understandable. This was a first. "Really. And if you go out the back way, you can take the alley. It'll be quicker."

Technically, that wasn't true. I'd tested it once, and the routes were equal. I didn't want her to go back out there, though. In fact, the farther away she could get, the better.

Luckily, she didn't question me. She shoved the money into her back jeans pocket. "Thanks, Boo. Want me to bring you back something?"

One of my imported orange sodas would sure hit the spot, but Chef Glen refused to stock them. Apparently, I was the only customer who had ever requested it. "Just get yourself something. No rush coming back. Actually, take the rest of the day off."

I waited until Sissy had closed the back door behind her, then I waited another full minute before I stepped out.

The young man stood at the rack of packaged costumes. His back was to me, but those dark curls teasing the collar of his grease-stained work shirt confirmed what I had suspected.

"Hello, Darren. Did you come on your own?" I asked. "Or did your father send you?"

Wyatt's son turned slowly, deliberate as ever. "Now, why would he do that?"

Something sinister slithered in his gaze. Far too dark for someone who still looked like a college kid.

I crossed my arms and squared myself to him. "I'm not interested in playing games. Just tell me what you want."

He lifted the package. "I'm getting ready for Halloween, like everybody else. I've always wanted to be a"—he turned the package around and squinted at the name on the plastic—"Ultra Deluxe Wolfman."

"I find that hard to believe."

"You want to know why I'm here? I heard you visited my dad today."

I sighed. Had it only been that morning? It felt so long ago. "I saw him. What about it?"

His razor-sharp stare faltered. His gaze dipped before rising again. "How was he?"

Was that a trick question? "He was fine. Tired, maybe. I can't imagine it's easy to sleep in a place like that."

"No, and not so close to... tomorrow night."

The full moon. Was that why he was here?

"I'm aware of the concern," I said cautiously.

His jaw tensed. "I heard you're calling a Midnight Council meeting."

"My sister and I are, yes. Did she call you?"

"No, that's why I'm here. I want to be there."

"Are you sure your dad would want that? He seems to prefer to keep his distance." There were plenty of us in the supernatural community who preferred that as well.

"When my dad returns, we'll follow his rules. Until then, the pack follows mine, and I say we'll be there."

I threw up my hands. "Fine. I'll see what I can do."

He scoffed and slid his fingers over his thin lips. "Look, I am coming to your little party, whether you like it or not. Seven o'clock in the back of the hardware shop, right?"

He waited for me to argue, but when I didn't, he took his wallet from his back pocket and pulled out a stack of bills, peeling off a few twenties that he left on the shelf beside him. He tucked the Wolfman costume under his arm. "I'm also going to take this. It'll give the family a good laugh."

At least someone would have a good time.

As I watched him leave my shop, I considered running after him and begging him not to follow through on his threat. Convincing the community to help someone who had turned his back on us years ago was hard enough, but having his son there, with that giant chip on his shoulder, might make it impossible.

Chapter 18

Sweet Pea

"Guess who showed up at the shop today?"

The screen door slammed behind me as I entered the house, dropped my keys by the fern in the foyer, and found Kheppy curled up on her favorite chair. The comfy one covered in burgundy velour and cat hair.

She stretched, sat up, and glared at me.

"Why are you looking at me like that? Did Del forget to feed you again?"

We usually left a bowl of kibble next to Kheppy's water bowl, in case she became hungry during the day, but I'd never seen her touch the stuff. I didn't blame her. It smelled like dirty socks.

Her usual evening meal was a small portion of boiled chicken breast or fish, with some diced carrots or peas tossed in. Whatever we had in the fridge.

Since Del had turned vegan, she'd occasionally tried to withhold the chicken or fish. It had not gone well.

When my sister tried to add tofu or tempeh as an alternative, Kheppy took matters into her own hands—or paws?—and satisfied her appetite with a stray rodent or bird she caught outside and dragged onto the porch.

I would scold her for making a mess, but she would just shrug and say something to the effect of "drastic times eat drastic measures."

Of course, it made no sense, but I knew what she meant. Since I'd told Del I wouldn't clean up any more of Kheppy's outside "meals," my sister had resigned herself to the cat's carnivorous ways. Unless she was trying to change them again.

Del's old Civic was back in the driveway with its new set of tires, so I knew she was home. The smell of something delicious in the kitchen was another dead giveaway. I pushed through the swinging door to see what she had in the works.

"Hey, are you in here? We had an interesting visitor—" I stopped the second I entered the kitchen and saw my sister sitting at the breakfast table with a cup of tea and her own interesting visitor.

That would explain why Kheppy hadn't muttered a word to me. As difficult as she could be sometimes, she was good about staying mum when others were around.

At the sight of me, Delphine jumped up and rushed to cut me off. "Boo, you're home! Look who dropped in while I was whipping up some gumbo!"

I could only see the visitor's back, but I would know Sissy's head of ginger-blond hair anywhere.

"If she invited you to stay for dinner, be warned. It's vegan gumbo. So, manage your expectations." Even though the house smelled wonderful, I'd been tricked by Delphine's vegan substitutes before and knew delicious smells did not always result in tasty food.

"Oh, Boo," Delphine slapped my arm playfully—though a little harder than usual. "I'm making both. Vegan for me. Andouille sausage and chicken for you. Happy?"

Actually, I was. Her chicken and sausage gumbo was my absolute favorite dish, and I breathed more deeply knowing those savory scents weren't a trick.

Delphine's hand was still on my elbow as she continued, "We've been having tea and some wonderful little orange cream cupcakes. Luna's recipe. You should join us."

It wasn't like I could refuse. My sister practically shoved me into an empty seat. But why was Sissy here, having tea with my sister? It had only been a couple of hours since I had sent her off for her fancy coffee.

A gut-punch of a thought struck me. I'd assumed she'd left right away. Had she hung around? Had she eavesdropped on my conversation with Darren?

My stomach did a somersault. If she *had* stuck around, she might have been confused by what she'd heard. I'd been careful, though. Hadn't I?

As doubt churned through me, she turned to me, and my heart stopped at the sight of those puffy, bloodshot eyes and the tissue clutched beneath her freckled little nose.

This. Was. Bad.

I planted my hands firmly on the table to steady myself as a wave of disorientation passed through me.

My sister, bless her, immediately noticed my distress. She leaned over and whispered, "Do you need a pill?"

She still believed blood pressure pills worked on an as-needed basis, despite my explanations. I shook my head.

When I composed myself, I reached for Sissy's knee to pat it. "My dear, I am so sorry."

Before I could continue my mea culpa, my sister patted my back. To Sissy, it might have appeared like she was consoling me, but I knew it was her gentle way of shutting me up.

"Sissy came here to speak with you, Boo. Something has been weighing on her that she needs to share with you. Something quite important."

I leaned back, puzzled. "All right. Whatever it is, dear, you can tell me anything." I braced, waiting for her to accuse me of keeping secrets from her. Secrets that were unfairly kept from her and which I had no right to with-hold. I had betrayed her on a deep, probably unforgivable level, and the pain of that was almost more than I could bear.

Sissy blew her nose into her rumpled tissue. My sister nudged the box closer to her, urging her to take a fresh one, which she ignored.

"I don't know how to say this." Sissy's voice cracked, her eyes shut, and the tissue flew back to her nose.

"Take your time, sweet pea," my sister said in her most soothing, most reassuring voice. "It's all right. You are among friends. Nothing will change that."

As Sissy blew again into that soggy tissue, I cut a questioning glance at Delphine, who returned a look that was the bulging eyeball version of "buckle up, buttercup."

Curiosity replaced the guilt burning within me. Then curiosity sank into dread.

What could possibly be so bad?

My mind raced through possibilities: Had there been another ordering mistake? Were a thousand witches' hats about to wind up at my front door?

Or had I upset her somehow?

Oh no. My dread plunged deeper into a don't-turn-off-the-lights, don't-go-to-the-basement-alone kind of fear.

What was the worst possible thing she could say to me?

She'd taken another job. She was leaving the Boo-tique.

It was a good thing I was already sitting because my heart was about to pound right out of my chest. Maybe I *should* take one of my stupid blood pressure pills.

I was pretty sure I needed something because my cheeks and throat burned, my heart raced, and the smell of savory goodness coming from the pots on the stove was turning my stomach upside down.

My sister must have seen my condition was going from bad to worse because she leaned forward and said to Sissy, "My dear, please. You'll feel better once it's out."

Sissy pulled the tissue away from her face and took a deep breath.

I tried to do the same. Big-girl panties and all that. I'd managed before I hired her. Not as well, but I had. And I could always hire another clerk. Right?

Sissy sniffled and swallowed. Then, she finally lifted her gaze to meet mine.

I clenched, bracing for the worst.

"Boo," she said in a shaky voice, "I haven't told you the truth about what happened that day in the store."

"Wait, what?"

My sister's hand flew up to shush me. She already knew what was coming next, and she wanted me to let Sissy finish.

When I stopped, Delphine made a gesture to Sissy, letting her know she should continue.

Sissy nodded and swallowed again. Then she took a deep breath and closed her eyes. "Boo, I killed Isabelle Blake."

Chapter 19

Truth Bomb

Sɪssʏ's ʟɪᴘs ᴡᴇʀᴇ ᴍᴏᴠɪɴɢ, but the words didn't add up. Ever since she'd dropped that truth bomb, the world had tilted sideways. Across the kitchen table, Delphine reached out and wrapped her hands around Sissy's trembling ones—calm as can be, like she hadn't just been hit with a blow to the heart. I didn't know how she managed it. I was still trying to breathe.

And I couldn't get past those four particular words—*I killed Isabelle Blake*. They kept looping through my brain like a record needle stuck in a groove.

"Wait," I said, interrupting whatever Sissy was trying to explain. "What do you mean you killed her? You weren't even there. You went to the hardware store."

Sissy chewed her lip. "I did leave. You're right. But I forgot my purse, so I went back. When I was in the office, I heard you at the door. At least, I thought it was you." Her gaze dropped to her lap. "But it was her."

"Isabelle? She came to the shop?" I asked.

Sissy's glance darted to Delphine, who nodded with reassurance.

139

"Go ahead, dear," my sister said. "It's all right."

"But I'd locked the door. I'm sure I did," I blurted.

Sissy nodded, sadness pulling at the corners of her eyes. "She was pounding on the glass. I tried to tell her we weren't open, but she begged me to let her in. She said she had something to tell me. I should have known better."

"Did she attack you?" That had to be what happened. It was the only reasonable explanation.

My heart dropped when Sissy shook her head.

"Let her tell it," my sister said, turning her soothing ministrations to me. She reached over and rubbed the back of my arm, trying to keep me calm.

She was right. I needed to shut my mouth and let Sissy explain in her own way. With all that shifting, twitching, and sniffling the girl was doing, she was clearly struggling.

I nodded at my sister and squeezed her hand in silent understanding. We both knew staying quiet wasn't easy for me, but I had to try.

Kheppy, who had wandered over to her water bowl, must have been following our silent exchange because she made her way to me and brushed her soft gray fur against my ankles.

Then, before I could stop her, she jumped onto my lap and curled into a ball. When our eyes met, she meowed softly, something she only did under extreme circumstances when strangers were around and she couldn't use her natural voice.

Apparently, Kheppy believed this to be an extreme circumstance.

I couldn't argue, and I welcomed her soft feline presence. When I rubbed the spot between her ears and made her purr, that soothing vibration melted the tension in my knees. I'd always wondered if this was one of Kheppy's unique abilities, or if every cat had the power to make the world feel like a better place. Even this moment—messy and painful as it was—suddenly felt a little less awful.

"I'm sorry, Sissy," I said in a calmer, working-toward-relaxed voice. "Please go ahead."

My shop clerk blew her nose into another tissue, wadded it up, and placed it on the pile accumulating on the table beside her.

"I told her we weren't open and that she should come back later. But then..." Sissy grimaced like she was about to cry, then swallowed the emotion. "She said, 'Do you know who I am?'"

As much as I wanted to jump in and ask what Isabelle had meant, I didn't. I kept rubbing Kheppy's head and telling myself to stay silent.

"I told her, of course I did, that she ran the shop across the street. Then she just stared at me, like she didn't believe me. It was so weird. She really gave me the creeps."

I wanted to ask Sissy to elaborate, but Kheppy meowed again and kneaded my thigh with her front paws. My little friend was doing everything in her power to keep me calm and quiet.

The tension must have been getting to Delphine, because she leaned over the table, and in her most gentle voice, she said, "Tell Boo what Isabelle said next. It's important."

Sissy gave her a pleading look. She didn't want to do it, and it broke my heart because I already knew what was coming next.

As much as I wanted to spare her the pain, my instincts told me I couldn't. She needed to do this. She needed to face the truth.

Sissy straightened in her seat and curled her fingers into fists on the table. "That woman said she was my mother. My birth mother."

The way her gaze darted to me, I knew she expected to see shock or amazement on my face. What she probably saw was despair, because that's what I felt. For what that woman had put her through as a baby and what learning the truth in this awful way was doing to her now. That revelation must have shaken her so deeply it pushed her to violence.

I touched her arm, which pressed Kheppy in my lap, but the sweetheart didn't even balk. "It wasn't fair of her to do that to you, Sissy. She had no right."

The pained expression on the young woman's face turned to puzzlement. "It isn't true, Boo. She was lying. She's not my mother."

I pulled back and recalibrated. "She's not?"

Kheppy jumped to the floor, probably sensing this conversation was about to take an uncomfortable turn.

"You know my parents. That woman was a lunatic. After she said she was my mother, she started raving about you. About how you're a bad influence and how I needed to get away from you because you're one of *them*."

"One of who?" I asked.

"How should I know? I told you, the woman was bonkers."

I couldn't rule that out, but I also couldn't rule out the possibility Isabelle Blake knew something about the supernatural community.

"So, you don't believe she's really your mother, but you killed her?" Delphine asked.

Leave it to my sister to get the conversation back on track. And the more I thought about it, the less sense Sissy's story made.

"You didn't see her," Sissy said. "She came after me. I tried to get her to leave, but she refused and kept saying all those awful things about Boo and claiming to be my mother. She said I should go with her for my own good. All kinds of bizarre things like that."

"Did she get violent?" I asked. That was the only explanation that made sense. It was the only thing that would justify Sissy's actions.

"Yeah," Sissy said, her face flushed with emotion as she mentally relived what had to have been a harrowing ordeal. "She kept pulling me. My arms, my hair, anything she could grab. She was out of control."

"That sounds awful," I said, trying to understand how it had escalated. "Did she have a weapon?"

The police hadn't found anything, at least to my knowledge, but it was possible, and it could strengthen Sissy's defense.

My shop clerk shook her head. "Just her hands. She kept grabbing me. That's why I pushed her. We were standing near the door, and she came at me, so I pushed her away and ran. I heard her fall, but I thought she would get up again, so I kept running. I just wanted to get away."

Sissy had pushed Isabelle, who must have stumbled and fallen into the cauldron. That's how she'd ended up face first in the green goo. She must have struck her head on the way in, lost consciousness, and drowned.

"What happened was awful," I said, "but it sounds like self-defense to me." And if Sissy didn't want to believe Isabelle was her mother, I wasn't about to press the issue.

"Do you think I should go to the police?" Sissy asked, her eyes welling with fresh tears.

That was a good question. On one hand, the longer she hid the truth, the guiltier she appeared. But on the other hand, I wanted to get her a good lawyer, so she didn't end up sitting in jail like Wyatt Landon.

"Not just yet," I said, deciding legal representation should be the first item on the agenda.

Delphine kept looking at her watch and acting twitchy.

"What? You don't agree?" I asked her sharply.

My sister shook her head. "It's not that. I do agree, but I'm afraid we're going to be late to our"—she gave me a long, pointed look—"appointment."

The Midnight Council. I'd completely forgotten about it. I checked the digital clock on the microwave. My sister was right. Even if we left this minute, we'd still be late.

Sissy rubbed her face. "I'm so sorry. You need to leave, and here I am bawling my eyes out."

"Not at all, Sissy." I touched her shoulder as I set Kheppy on the floor and rose from my seat. "I'm glad you came. We both are, and we will figure this out. I promise. Let me think about it tonight. You go home, don't do anything rash or tell anyone else, and we'll decide what to do in the morning. Can we do that?"

When my sister rose from her chair, Sissy did the same. Delphine went to the stove to give the pots a stir and moved them into the oven to keep warm.

I led Sissy to the living room, where she scooped up her purse and promised to go home and rest. "Whatever you think I should do, I'll do it. I trust you, Boo."

She turned those wide, innocent eyes on me and pulled me in for a bear hug. I returned the embrace, holding her tight, like I might never get another chance.

Depending on how tonight's meeting went, I wasn't sure I would.

Chapter 20

Utter Mayhem

Delphine and I knocked on the back door of Howard's hardware store twice before anyone answered it.

"It's about time," Merle grumbled as he waved us inside and frowned at the cat carrier Delphine gripped like a large briefcase at her side. "What's that?"

"Kheppy refused to be left behind," I said, rolling my eyes to show it was already a sore point. At least Kheppy had promised to behave herself.

Merle shrugged and hurried us down the corridor, past the washroom and the manager's office to the storage room.

All the crates and cardboard boxes had been pushed against the wall to create space for a couple of dozen folding chairs arranged theater style, facing the table where the elders sat. There was Howard in his usual coveralls, of course, representing the psychics and mediums, sitting next to Neal Glory, who I almost didn't recognize because he'd bleached his jet-black hair platinum blond since Isabelle's murder.

He'd told me once, extreme makeovers helped merfolk cope with tragedy, but I suspected it was a personal choice because I'd never seen another merman change his look as drastically or as frequently as Neal did. Neal was also the only mer hairstylist I knew, but if he wanted to blame his flair for the dramatic on his sea-born roots, who was I to argue?

The last member of the supernatural triumvirate was Cornelia Sloane, an imposing figure in her dark, tailored suit, and not just because she had the kind of sharply angled bone structure and penetrating gaze that characterized most vampires—at least the ones I'd met. She was the publisher of the local newspaper and ruled it with the iron grip of a medieval monarch. Which she might well have been at one time. No one really knew her story. But then, vampires tended to be tight-lipped about the past.

She turned that frightening gaze on me and Delphine as we settled into the seats Jemma and Willa had saved for us near the back.

"So good of you to join us, ladies," Cornelia said, running one long and narrow finger across her forehead like she was guiding a stray lock into place, but there was no need. That sleek chignon was always perfectly smooth. "From Delphine's message, I thought this was an emergency. A false alarm, I presume?"

Her insinuation that we'd called everyone together under false pretenses set off a round of grumbling, which is exactly what she'd intended.

Delphine leaned toward me and muttered, "Cranky Cornelia is in fine form tonight."

"I'm sorry." Cornelia touched her ear. "Delphine, did you say something?"

Delphine gave her a saccharine grin. "Just happy to see everyone. It's been a long time for some of us."

I bit my lip to hide my amusement. A vampire's hearing was even better than a werewolf's, so there was no way Cornelia hadn't heard what Delphine said.

Someone said under their breath, "Not long enough," and set off another round of murmurs.

I wasn't sure why until I noticed most of the people in the room were staring at someone sitting in the front row. A tall, dark-haired someone oozing wannabe alpha energy from every pore.

So, Darren had made good on his threat to attend the meeting.

If he had noticed any of the shady glances, he didn't show it. Or he didn't care, because he stood up and turned his back on the elders and addressed the rest of us.

"You all know by now that the police have locked up my dad and are accusing him of a crime he didn't commit. He's being framed, and we need to get him out of there, for his sake and for the sake of everyone in this room. Actually, for the sake of everyone whose life depends on privacy."

As he spoke, his voice grew louder and more forceful, like he was trying to project the confident leadership that came so naturally to his father.

It wasn't working.

At the elders' table, Howard shook his head as Darren spoke. Now he stood up. "You say your dad is being framed, but how do we know that's true? How do we know he didn't kill that woman?"

A woman named Claire who'd moved to town a few years ago and who I'd heard could see animal ghosts, which probably explained why she'd opened the town's only pet cemetery, stood, tossed back her waist-length, blond hair, and addressed Darren. "Why should we help you? I don't know you, I don't know your father, and as long as I've been here, the wolves have never once tried to help anyone but themselves."

A wave of nods and murmurs of agreement passed through the room.

"You can bicker all you want about what happened in the past, but it won't change the fact that if my father is still in that jail cell at midnight tomorrow, the consequences will expose us all. What do you think the police will do when they have to deal with a hungry werewolf? It's going to raise a lot of questions in this town, and you won't like what a full-scale investigation might turn up. Have you thought about that?"

The room remained silent for a long, tense moment. What would the normies do if they ever confronted a real-life werewolf?

Considering Wyatt Landon had a long history in this town, I had no doubt Darren was correct in saying an investigation could destroy our community.

The young man watched the crowd's weakening protest with a victorious glint in his eye. "And please know," he added with a smirk, "that if the wolves go down, we won't go down alone."

Merle had been standing at the back near the door, his hefty arms folded over his western-embroidered shirt. But now his face was red, and his index finger punched the air in Darren's direction as he swaggered toward the younger man. "So, you came here to threaten us? You're going to try to bully us into helping you free your dad? Well, that's a wolf for you. Always looking out for themselves. Who cares about anybody else?" He shook his head in disgust.

And he wasn't alone.

Darren sneered back at Merle. "You don't know what you're talking about, old man. You've been listening to that imaginary friend of yours for too long."

When Merle didn't back off, Darren's shoulders hunched, and he lurched forward, like he might take a swing. Everyone between them jumped from their seats. Some rushed to hold Darren. Some blocked Merle from advancing on the young man. The rest scurried out of the way.

It was utter mayhem, and if nobody stepped in, someone was going to get hurt. Or worse.

"Stop it! Stop it this instant!"

Everyone in the room froze and turned to look at the hysterical woman screaming in the back. Unfortunately, that hysterical woman was me.

Even Delphine looked up at me, her face caught between shock and horror. Kheppy's tail thumped against her carrier wall.

"What I mean to say is," I added in what I hoped was a more rational tone, "there is no need for this. Darren is right. His father deserves our help. Not just because he's part of our community—whether you agree with that or not—but because he is innocent. He did not kill Isabelle Blake."

Merle shook his head. "You're giving him the benefit of the doubt, Boo, and he doesn't deserve it."

"You're wrong, Merle. I know he didn't kill that woman because I know who did. We both do, don't we, Delphine?"

My sister had been staring at the floor, probably wishing she could disappear. But now she glanced up, first to me and then to everyone else.

She nodded slowly. "It's true. We do."

For a second, it was so quiet, you could hear a motorcycle engine revving in the distance.

"Who is it? Who tried to frame my father?" Darren demanded.

"She wasn't trying to frame anybody. She was only trying to defend herself. It was an accident. A terrible, fatal accident, and I'm going to do everything I can to be sure the authorities understand that."

That's when I spotted Beth Meyers at the edge of the crowd, sitting beside Opal. I smiled at Beth, delighted she'd finally embraced her place in the community. But then I realized what I was about to say.

Maybe she did too.

"Who is it, Boo?" she urged.

There was already pain in those wide brown eyes of hers. Was it her mother's intuition? Did she already know?

Then she closed her eyes and nodded. Yes, she knew the truth.

"It was my shop clerk, Sissy," I said to audible gasps. "She confessed to me and Delphine this evening. She told us everything."

Chapter 21
A Simple Solution

ONCE I'D EXPLAINED TO the Midnight Council what Sissy had confessed to Del and me, I braced for Beth Meyers's reaction. What mother could endure hearing such a horrible thing about her child, even if it was the truth?

I expected tears or screams or, at the very least, a hasty departure.

Instead, Beth straightened her shoulders and lifted her chin. "Anyone who knows Sissy," she said once the shock and whispers had died down, "knows my daughter doesn't have a mean bone in her body. If she killed Isabelle Blake, it had to be what Boo said it was. Self-defense or an accident. Maybe both. Whatever it was, we will figure it out, and we will deal with it. Right now, we have to decide how to help Wyatt."

I had to give the woman credit. She had tried to blame Wyatt during our earlier conversation, but now that she knew the truth, she was coming to his defense. Bravo, Mrs. Meyers.

When she caught Darren's eye, he straightened. "Yes. Exactly," he said, taking her cue. "We have to get my father out of jail before midnight tomorrow, or he won't stand a chance against the power of the full moon."

Merle wasn't sneering anymore, but he didn't look happy, either. He rubbed his palm against the back of his neck, then said, "Fine. Do you have a plan?"

Darren nodded. "A few of our guys have checked out the building. They say it wouldn't take much to bust through those walls."

Merle pinched the bridge of his nose. "You're proposing we break him out of jail? Seriously?"

"Well, yeah," Darren said with a shrug, as if it were the only logical answer. "We can use my dad's truck. The thing is huge. The jail's back wall is next to the parking lot, so if we drilled a few holes, inserted steel anchors that we chained to the hitch—"

"Hold up," Howard said, rising from his seat at the elders' table. "I'm not sure that's the way to go." He hiked up his denim overalls as he joined Merle, whose face had turned a deep crimson, his nostrils flaring like a racehorse. I imagined he was doing everything in his power not to shoot down Darren's idea.

Better to let Howard do it.

"Why not?" Darren shot back defensively.

"Don't you think the police would notice somebody trying to drill holes into their walls? I believe they'd have plenty of time to put a stop to that kind of thing before you could do any damage," Howard said.

"Not if one of the vampires rode shotgun," Darren quipped. "They could cast one of those woo-woo spells that make people do whatever they want."

Cranky Cornelia turned her evil eye on Darren. "That, young man, is not how a glamour works."

He whipped around and sneered at her. "Fine. Then maybe one of you could just walk into the jail and do your woo-woo spell on the guards. No truck, no fuss. Just a zombie guard or two willing to unlock the door and let my dad walk out a free man. We can make sure he's long gone before they come to their senses."

Cornelia stared at him so long and so hard, I wondered if she was trying to do that woo-woo, glamour business on him right then and there. It wouldn't surprise me. I didn't know much about the age-old rift between vampires and werewolves, but I knew that hatred and distrust ran deep.

"Was that your plan all along, wolf? To make a vampire do your bidding?" Cornelia exaggerated her enunciation so that Darren caught the flash of her fangs.

He did, and so did the rest of us, and we all knew when vampires flashed their fangs, they had every intention of using them.

"Hold on now," Merle said, stepping between Darren and Cornelia like a referee. "No one is going to do anyone else's bidding. Unless I'm mistaken, we've all agreed that getting Wyatt out of lockup is in everyone's best interest."

Several people nodded and murmured agreement, including me.

He continued. "If the humans discover a full-moon-crazed werewolf in their midst, you can bet it will set off alarm bells in this town, which could easily end our relatively peaceful existence here in Laguna Bay. Is that what you want?"

Merle was looking at Cornelia, and her smoldering gaze made it clear she didn't appreciate his implication. Merle held his ground and continued to wait for her to respond.

"It's a ridiculous question," she hissed back. "No one wants that. We also don't want to be bullied by..." She paused, letting our imaginations fill in the blank, until she said, "them," and jutted the sharp point of her chin at Darren. "I didn't want to resort to this, but you've forced my hand. As the Supernaturals Social Contract of 1908 states, disputes shall be decided by the eldest member of a clan, or where they concern two or more clans, the eldest member among them." She made a point of looking around, meeting and returning every gaze, before adding with a self-congratulatory grin, "I'm sure I don't have to remind anyone here that I am our eldest member."

We all knew that rule, yet it had been decades since anyone had invoked it. It had not been invoked for so long, it seemed almost crass to do so now.

But then, appearing crass never seemed to bother Cornelia.

"So, that's it then? She gets her way because she's old?" Darren wailed.

Merle looked at Howard. Howard looked at Chef Glen. Everyone else sank back in their chairs and shook their heads. No one thought it was an ideal system, but no one wanted to stir up more trouble, either.

"Excuse me."

Those two sharp words made everyone in the room turn back at Delphine and me. They'd assumed one of us had said it, but to my surprise, neither of us had. It was Kheppy.

I bent down to the carrier's metal grate door. "What are you doing?" I whispered. "Be quiet."

"Do you have something to add, Boo?" Merle asked.

He looked like he hoped I did, even as Cornelia aimed her evil eye at me.

I tried to laugh it off as if there had been a mistake. "No, it was—"

"It was I," Kheppy said even more loudly than before. "If you would let me out, I will explain."

Delphine whipped around and mouthed, "What do we do now?"

"I don't know," I mouthed back, and truly I didn't.

"Boo, please let me out."

Everyone had heard her, so there was no point in pretending the cat inside the carrier had not made the request. There was only one thing I could do, so I opened the door.

When it unlatched, Kheppy leaped out to the floor, then she jumped back on top of the carrier and glanced around like a queen reclaiming her throne.

"Good evening," she said. "Most of you may think you know me, but we have never been properly introduced. My name is Khepeset, immortal descendant of Bastet, former advisor to the greatest pharaohs of Upper and Lower Egypt, and once a beloved companion of the glorious Queen Cleopatra."

"Is this some kind of joke?" Darren's lips twisted in disgust.

Kheppy shot him a withering look. "Quiet, wolf. I am speaking."

He rolled his eyes, but everyone else watched Kheppy, curious where this was going.

I had to admit, I was curious too.

She'd hidden this side of herself from everyone but our closest friends. Why reveal her secret so publicly now?

"The vampire says she is the oldest among us, yet I must respectfully correct her. I had already served many pharaohs before the Mad Priest conjured the first vampire during the Second Dynasty."

Cornelia scoffed. "Impossible."

"Hardly," Kheppy said. "I know many things that are true, such as how the first of your kind was the result of the Mad Priest's experiments with the mummification process. Shall I show you?"

Before Cornelia could mask her curiosity, Kheppy crossed the room and leaped onto a stack of crates beside the vampire. "Look into my eyes," she said to Cornelia.

The woman turned with a shrug, as though she intended to say, "No, thank you," but once their gazes met, Cornelia went as limp as one of her own glamour victims.

We all watched Kheppy hold her in thrall.

"It's true," an awestruck Cornelia whispered once the spell broke and her clarity returned.

Kheppy rolled her shoulders and stretched her neck. "Do you still doubt I am your elder?"

It was the first time I had ever seen Cornelia bow her head. "I do not," she said. "I shall defer to you, Ancient One."

The cat tensed. "Khepeset will do." She turned to the rest of us. "First, this bickering must end. The threat to the community affects us all, but there is a simple solution."

"There is?" I didn't realize I'd asked the question aloud until everyone looked at me.

"Yes, Boo. There is," Kheppy said. "You will go to the police detective and tell him about Sissy."

Out of the corner of my eye, I caught Beth's arm move in protest. But she stopped herself, folded her arms across her chest, and let Kheppy finish.

"Tell them about Isabelle Blake's aggression, just as Sissy explained it to you. Tell them Sissy was protecting herself and that it was—how did you phrase it?—an accident. Does anyone disagree?"

Only shrugs and nods and silence followed. But then, who would dare to argue with an ancient cat who could tame Cranky Cornelia?

Chapter 22

Common Sense

"A LITTLE WARNING WOULD have been nice," I whispered to Kheppy as she stepped back into her carrier.

The three elders were still huddled at their table, whispering about who knows what, while most of the others had left. Delphine was a few paces away, talking to Beth. Consoling her, by the looks of it. That left me to deal with Kheppy.

"Warn you about what, exactly?" the cat asked.

"That you were going to announce to everyone who you are. Honestly, why now? After all this time?"

I expected a snarky retort, but instead, her little chest heaved a sigh.

"It was time," she said. "And it was needed. They would have talked and delayed and threatened one another until it was too late. Now, you can get with it."

Get with what? Oh. "You mean, get *on* with it."

Was she smiling at me? It was hard to tell in the carrier's shadows.

"Yes, whatever you want to say." She curled up into a gray ball of fur at the back of the plastic box and watched silently as I latched the door.

When I heard footsteps behind me, my instinct was to shush her. But there was no more need of that, at least not with anyone in this room. Before long, I expected word would spread to the other supernaturals too. Secrets didn't stay secret for long in our tight-knit community.

"Hey, Boo," Howard said gently as I finished securing the carrier's door. "Everything all right?"

That wasn't the Howard I knew. He sounded unsure of himself. I glanced back over my shoulder and found him frowning at the floor.

I turned in my chair to face him fully. "We're fine. But you don't look so good. What's going on?"

His gaze darted to Cornelia and Neal Glory, who were still deep in conversation, then stepped closer and whispered, "Can we talk outside?"

He certainly had my attention now. I glanced at Delphine, who was still consoling Beth while also watching me and Howard. I pointed to Kheppy's carrier and mouthed, "Watch her."

When she nodded, I turned back to Howard. "Sure. Let's take a walk."

He didn't stop until we were clear across his parking lot, standing in the soft amber glow of a streetlight. The nighttime mist had already rolled in off the ocean, and I regretted not bringing my denim jacket with me. Instead,

I folded my arms over my chest and rubbed my palms over my goose-bumpy skin to warm myself.

"What's on your mind, Howard?" I didn't want to rush the guy, but California gals like me weren't built for the cold.

Finally, he looked up from the tips of his work boots. "It's Sissy."

He wasn't going to make this easy, was he? "What about her? What couldn't you say inside?" Where it was warm, and I didn't have to tense my jaw to keep my teeth from chattering.

"She came to the hardware store right before they found that woman. Do you remember?"

"Yes, of course, I remember. What does that have to do with it?"

He ran his hand over the scattering of gray hairs he had combed over his freckled scalp. "Sissy couldn't have done what you said she did. I just don't believe it."

Howard was a kind, sweet soul. It didn't surprise me he didn't want to believe Sissy could be capable of killing anyone, even a wicked birth mother who had abandoned her.

"Look," I said, "once the authorities realize it was self-defense, she won't have anything to worry about. If she explains it to them like she explained it to me, they'll see it was an accident. Sissy didn't mean to hurt that woman, and there has to be intent to convict someone of murder, right?"

His forehead wrinkled with doubt. "I'm no lawyer, but I'm pretty sure it doesn't work that way."

I wasn't a lawyer either, but it sounded like the kind of thing they always said on crime shows.

"Regardless," I added, "once she tells the police how that woman was hounding her, they'll understand."

"Are you sure about that?"

He obviously wasn't. "Yeah. It's common sense."

"I wish I had your optimism." He shoved his hands into his pockets and gazed off toward the ocean, even though nothing was visible beyond the streetlights and boardwalk lights that rimmed Main Beach.

Was I being unrealistic? Now I wasn't sure.

"What are you getting at, Howard?" If he had a better plan, I wanted to hear it.

"I don't think things happened the way Sissy says they happened. I think she's covering for someone."

"Why do you think that?" I asked, intrigued. Did he suspect Beth Meyers, as I had?

"You said Sissy pushed Isabelle away when Isabelle grabbed her." He held his hands in front of himself as if he were holding a woman by the shoulders.

"That's right. That's what she told me."

"And she said Isabelle must have stumbled backward and fallen into the cauldron when Sissy ran out the back to get away from her."

"Right. That's what she said."

"Try coming at me, like Isabelle went after Sissy," he said.

163

"C'mon, Howard. I'm not going to attack you."

"You won't hurt me. Just pretend. Come at me the way you think Isabelle went after Sissy."

I could argue, or I could do it and be done with it. I chose the latter. Holding up both hands, I pretended to rush at him.

When I was close enough, he shoved me back. Not hard, but hard enough that I stumbled.

"Okay, what does that prove?" I asked when I got my bearings.

"It proves Isabelle might have stumbled, and she might even have fallen, but how in the world would she have stumbled while stepping up to the cauldron and then fallen headfirst into the thing? Think about it."

I didn't want to think about it, because the instant he posed the question, I could picture it, and it was impossible. There was no way Isabelle could have stumbled *up* to the cauldron.

Not without help.

"You don't think it was an accident, do you?" I asked. Had I ruled out Beth too quickly? I wasn't sure, but Howard was right about Sissy's version of events. It didn't add up.

"All I'm saying is, I don't think it was an accident," he said.

"So, it was Beth," I said grimly. How had she fooled me?

"No, not Beth," he said.

"Huh? You lost me."

He looked away and ran his palm over those sparse gray hairs. "Sissy showed up at the hardware store after her encounter with Isabelle, right?"

"Right. We've established that. Did she say something to you?"

"Not exactly, but that boyfriend of hers came in while she was waiting for me to get the dry ice from the back. I heard them talking."

When he paused, I wanted to throttle him. I would have done it too, if he hadn't looked queasy.

"C'mon, what did they say?" I urged when I couldn't stand it any longer.

He sighed. "That kid sounded so pleased with himself. So smug. He came in, and the first thing he said to Sissy was, 'I saw what that woman did to you, but she won't bother you again. I took care of it.'"

"What did he mean by that?" I knew what I thought he meant, but there was no room for assumptions here. I had to hear it.

"I didn't know at the time, but now..." He threw up his hands as if the answer was obvious.

"Why didn't you say something in there?" I jabbed a finger at the hardware store's back door. "Why did you let me blame Sissy if you knew this?" Anger clashed with frustration, and under it all was a surprising wave of relief—Sissy hadn't hurt Isabelle.

"I couldn't say anything without proof. If Sissy's claiming she did it, it's because she's covering for that boy. I don't think he deserves it—and I don't think he deserves her—but that's not my call."

"That's ridiculous." My voice came out sharper than I meant. "Maybe he threatened her. Maybe he brainwashed her. Did you think of that?"

The heat in my chest told me exactly what I had to do. "You can sit on what you know and do nothing, Howard, but I can't. I'm going to prove Ryan killed Isabelle—and make sure no one else pays for a crime they didn't commit."

Chapter 23

Wink and a Smile

I DIDN'T SAY A word as I drove Delphine and Kheppy home. The entire ride, I mentally played through ways I could confront Ryan. None of them seemed likely to get me a confession—just arrested for harassment.

"Are you going to tell me what that secret meeting with Howard was about?" Delphine said when I pulled into our driveway. "Or do I have to guess?"

"I have heard of these guessing games," Kheppy said, perking up from where she was sleeping on the back seat beside her plastic carrier since she'd demanded to be freed from it the instant we were in the car. "Let me try. Is it bigger than a shoebox?"

"It isn't a game," I snapped, then sighed. "I'm sorry. I'm just tired."

Nine o'clock was the time I usually got ready for bed, but Delphine deserved an answer. She had a right to know what Howard had told me. Kheppy did too, for that matter.

My feline friend had sacrificed a lot tonight. As long as I'd known her—heck, as long as my parents and my grandparents had known her—she had protected the secret of her origin. It made sense to hide it from the normies, but she had been adamant about keeping it from the other supernaturals too.

I figured she had her reasons, but now that she'd broken her own rule, I wondered if she realized the magnitude of what she had done. At the very least, she deserved to know what Howard had said.

"Anyone up for a pot of tea?" I asked, trying to lighten the mood as I pulled my key from the car's ignition. "It's a long story, and I know I could use a cup."

"I could be talked into lemon chamomile. Or maybe peppermint," Del said as she worked her way out of the low bucket seat.

"I need something a little stronger than that," I said as I waddled through the front door with Kheppy in one arm and her carrier in the other. "Actually, make that a lot stronger."

"Sissy lied to us," Delphine said for the second time since we'd settled at the kitchen table to sip our tea.

The first time, it had been a question, like my sister couldn't believe she'd heard me correctly. This time, it was a statement. A resigned acceptance that, for whatever reason, Sissy had misled us to protect that boyfriend of hers.

"She's young," I said, flicking the tag tethered to the tea bag submerged in my mug. "She probably thinks she's in love, and you know how she is. That girl would give someone the shirt off her back if she thought they needed it. Not a selfish bone in her body."

"What if she goes to prison? Do you know what happens to girls like her in places like that?" Del asked.

Kheppy had been snoozing on the chair between us, but that woke her up. She poked her head above the tabletop and eyed us both. "What happens to girls like Sissy in prison?"

"Nothing," I shot back. "Because Sissy is not going to prison."

"How do you know?" My sister was taking the news worse than I'd expected. She was usually the one who looked on the brighter side of things, but tonight she was all doom and gloom.

Before I could answer, someone knocked on our door.

"Who do you suppose that is?" Delphine asked, obviously waiting for me to get up because she wasn't budging.

I was hoping it was Willa. If ever there was a time I needed that woman's wisdom, it was now.

When I opened the door, Merle was standing on my porch.

"Howdy, Boo." He pulled off his cowboy hat and gave me one of those concerned looks of his.

"Am I in trouble?" I asked.

"No." He scoffed, slightly amused. Then he frowned. "Why? What did you do?"

"Nothing yet. We're having tea. May I interest you in a cup?" I stepped aside and invited him in.

"No coffee?" He waved to Delphine at the kitchen table.

"No coffee," I confirmed.

"Tea's fine, then. As long as it's not one of those barely there, fruity things."

"I'll see what I can do," I said as I went to the kettle.

Delphine waved her hand at Kheppy to shoo her off the table's third chair so Merle could sit there.

Kheppy glared at her but rose and was about to jump to the floor when Merle stepped in. "No, no. I can see the seat is occupied. I prefer to stand anyway."

"Thank you, Merle." Kheppy regarded him for a moment before adding, "I appreciate your consideration. As it happens, I was about to leave. I have a feeling tomorrow will be a long day, so I would like to turn it in."

I bit my lip to stop myself from correcting her. This wasn't the time.

She jumped to the floor, gave Merle a last look and a slight nod, wished Delphine and me a good night, and sauntered back to my bedroom, where I assumed she'd make herself comfortable on my bed, as was her nightly habit.

When she was gone, Merle sucked in a deep breath and took the vacated seat. "A talking cat. That will take some getting used to."

He had no idea.

A moment later, I handed him a steaming mug with two tea bags of our blackest tea submerged in it. "It's strong now, but if you let it steep another minute, it'll get stronger."

He sipped. "Oh, this is good. Not coffee, mind you, but good."

"Oh, you two," Delphine said, shaking her head. "You know all that caffeine will mess with your system, right?"

"We're grownups," I said. "We'll be fine. Do you want a refill?"

She shook her head.

"I suppose you're wondering why I stopped by," Merle said, as he toyed with the tea bag strings. "I wanted to be sure you're not worried about tomorrow." After a brief pause, he added, "I can go with you to talk to the detective, if it would make things easier."

"Thank you," I said. "I don't think it will help, though."

That glimmer of hope in his eyes dimmed.

"Right, it was just a thought," he added quickly. "I know you can handle it. You can handle anything."

Was that what he thought? Because I sure wasn't convinced. Then again, he had always been my biggest cheerleader. No matter what, he was always on my side, and he always wanted to help. Heck, he was even fixing my pipes and wiring.

I set my hand lightly on his.

He looked at me, confused.

"You know," Del said, pushing her chair back from the table. "I think Kheppy has the right idea. It's already past my bedtime. No, no, you two enjoy your tea. Goodnight. I'll see you in the morning, Boo."

The lingering smile she gave Merle made me think she was about to say something inappropriate. Instead, she gave him a wink and a smile, which was almost as bad.

"I'm sorry about that," I said after she left the room. "She knows we're just friends. She just enjoys making things awkward."

He pulled his hand away from mine and rested it in his lap. "Right. Of course." Then he sort of scoffed and chuckled at the same time.

I had no idea what to say next, so I jumped back to what we'd been talking about before Del made things uncomfortable.

"I do appreciate your offer," I said. "It just won't be needed. I no longer believe Sissy killed Isabelle."

It took a lot of explaining, but eventually Merle agreed with me.

"Doesn't surprise me," he said. "That boyfriend of hers gave me the creeps. Didn't I say that? The guy is trouble." He nodded and twirled the tea bag strings around his index finger.

"You were right. I should have seen it too. Hopefully, it will be sorted out tomorrow. Once I tell the detective what we know, he'll see through Sissy's story, and more importantly, release Wyatt."

Merle sighed.

"What's wrong?" I asked. "Why are you frowning like that?"

"I just hope it's enough," he said. "I heard the mayor talking to that new detective at the station today. She's pushing to get Wyatt transferred to the county jail, so she can put out a big press release about it. With the election coming up, she wants to show voters she's tough on crime."

"That's ridiculous. Before Isabelle, the worst crimes in this town were jaywalking and parking violations, and those only happen with the beach crowd."

"She says it'll help her campaign."

"Are you kidding me? How much help does she need? She's running unopposed."

"Maybe not," he said.

"Maybe not what?"

"She might have an opponent. The city clerk told her someone had requested the paperwork, and the deadline to submit is Monday. There's still time for somebody to get in the race."

"Who is it?"

He shrugged. "Mallory doesn't know. The city clerk doesn't even know. The request came anonymously."

I sat back in my chair. "So, Mallory is on a campaign warpath, and poor Wyatt is going to suffer for it."

Merle nodded sadly.

"I never thought I'd say this, but I feel bad for the guy."

"Me too. And imagine what will happen if he transforms while he's at the county jail?"

All that attention will be devastating. For Wyatt, certainly, but also for those of us who depend on keeping our private lives private.

"There's got to be a way to stop her from doing that," I said. "And I'm going to find it or die trying."

Chapter 24

Holding Swords

As much as I hated to admit it, Del might have been right about the tea. The weight of the day hit me soon after Merle left, and I'd gone to bed, exhausted. But despite the weariness in my limbs and behind my eyes, I could not fall asleep. Instead, I'd been staring at the ceiling for what felt like hours.

Kheppy became so fed up with my tossing and turning she'd abandoned me almost immediately. I didn't blame her. I wasn't good company.

Relief would only come once I figured out how to stop Sissy from sabotaging herself. The girl was innocent, and all I had to do was prove it.

What I wanted to do was confront Ryan and force a confession out of him. I'd come up with at least a dozen scenarios: confront him at his apartment, confront him on the street, confront him at work.

Every time I mentally played out an encounter, it always ended the same way. He'd simply deny it. It would be my word against his, and with Sissy on his side, who would believe me?

Knowing I was right and knowing it might not matter was maddening.

Too maddening to stay in bed and fret about it, I decided.

If I couldn't sleep, there was no point in trying, so I got up and shuffled to the kitchen.

That late-night tea might be the reason I was still awake, but it was also the only thing I wanted. Some warm comfort in these cold, dark hours. I filled the kettle and set it on the stove to heat while I pulled the tea packets and a fresh mug from the cupboard.

"May I join you?"

Kheppy's little voice gave me a start. She sat on the kitchen table watching me, her eyes glinting in the dim light.

"I did not mean to scare you," she added sweetly.

"It's not you. I just can't sleep. This whole terrible mess has me on edge. Of course, you can join me. Honestly, I could use a friend."

"Friend." She said the word as if she were deciding whether she liked the sound of it. "We are friends, aren't we?"

"Of course, we are, Khep. We've always been friends. You were my very first friend. Do you remember?"

"I remember."

Even before Del was born, there was Kheppy. That cat followed my toddler self everywhere, and my parents allowed it. Maybe even encouraged it. I suppose they knew I'd eventually become her caretaker.

Which reminded me that one day, Del and I would have to pass that honor on to someone else.

But not today.

Today I had other burdens to bear.

"As your friend, may I ask what is bothering you?" She was still sitting, still watching me.

"I don't know how to help Sissy." That was it in a nutshell. I'd been going around and around in my mind about how to get Ryan to admit what he'd done, but all I really wanted to do was save that innocent young woman.

"Is it because she makes you think of Lila?"

"What kind of question is that?" Kheppy's reference to my daughter struck me like a freight train. The box of tea slipped from my fingers, and I scrambled to pick it up from the floor. "I'm sorry. I didn't mean that."

"Yes, I know. She makes me think of Lila too. Of what she could have been like at that age."

Why hadn't I made that connection to my daughter before? We rarely spoke of Lila. Del and Kheppy knew it pained me to remember how she'd been kept away from me, how she'd lived most of her life in another part of the world without me. Out of my reach and out of my life.

I had high hopes when she had returned with her own daughter. Luna was such a vibrant, happy child, and through her, I hoped I was seeing some of what I had missed with Lila. I tried in so many ways to make up for that lost time, but it was never enough. When she left Luna with Del and me without telling us even where she was going, I knew I couldn't fix whatever had broken between us.

At least Luna stayed. At least I had my granddaughter.

Kheppy jumped to the floor, then leaped to the counter and sniffed my tea. "Perhaps you do not know what to do because your head and your heart cannot agree."

I put the bag into the mug and poured the near-boiling water over it. "If you're trying to say I'm a muddled mess, then yeah—you've hit the nail on the head."

"I will not hit your head, Boo. Violence is never the answer."

"No, I suppose it isn't." It took every ounce of self-control I had to get the words out while sucking back a grin. She was the sweetest little creature alive, even if her grasp of modern language wasn't perfect.

"May I make a suggestion?" she asked.

"Certainly." I lifted the mug to my nose and breathed in the spicy aroma before taking a sip of the rich cinnamon blend.

"You used to consult the cards when you needed direction."

"Used to. That's the key part of that sentence," I grumbled.

"Is it worth giving them another try? No harm if they do not." When I didn't respond, she added, "If they had truly abandoned you, they would not have warned Del about the judges' early arrival."

Had they actually helped? If I hadn't left the shop that morning, would Isabelle still be alive? Would everything be different?

No, the cards held no answers for me. "I couldn't even if I wanted to, Khep," I said. "I don't know where my cards are."

"Del found them," Kheppy said. "She put them here in case you needed them."

I flipped on the kitchen light and saw Kheppy was right. The familiar blue velvet bag that held my cards was sitting in the middle of the kitchen table. When had my sister dug it out from the bottom drawer in my room, where I'd stashed it under a pile of old sweaters?

Kheppy leaped back onto the table. "It would be little trouble to ask them."

I leaned against the counter and sipped my tea. "You two are in cahoots, aren't you? Did you plan this?"

"No cahoots, but we think it might help."

"Well, no, thank you." I turned around and stared out the window at the night sky and the nearly full moon. A not-so-subtle reminder that time was running out to save Wyatt. "Del can ask them if that's what she wants to do."

I waited for Kheppy to argue with me, but she sat silently for a long moment. Then she said, "I have often wondered about the tarot."

"What do you mean?" Was she trying to trick me into doing a reading? It didn't sound like it, but I was curious.

"Perhaps the cards do not speak at all. Perhaps they only reflect."

"Like a mirror?"

Kheppy nodded. "Yes, somewhat like a mirror."

I considered it. "So, you think you only see in them what you already know within yourself?"

Her tiny, feline shoulders shrugged. "It is only a thought. What do you think?"

I couldn't deny it rang true.

But then, what did that say about that reading all those years ago?

Kheppy watched as my mental pendulum swung between agreement and doubt.

"Turn one card," Kheppy said. "And we will see."

"I did that already. With Del's cards. Remember? That's why I went to see Wyatt."

"And it helped," Kheppy said.

Had it? "I think the jury is still out on that one."

"Then try again."

"Okay. One card to prove this is all nonsense."

Kheppy gave me a look that made me wish I'd kept my mouth shut.

"Fine," I said. "One card."

I put down my teacup, grabbed the velvet satchel, and fished out the deck. It was strange, holding my deck again. It had been so long, but the weight of the cards, the smoothness of them, were still so familiar.

"Just one card," Kheppy said in her encouraging way.

I settled into a chair and shuffled the deck three times, then split it three times and shuffled again. When my hand rested on the top card, I took a slow, deep breath before turning it face up on the table.

Seven of Swords.

The image of a man sneaking away with an armful of swords, afraid of being caught. Deceit. Dishonesty. Violence. The usual interpretations flooded my mind and gave me a chill.

What caught my eye, though, were his hands. He was holding the swords at their sharp, pointy ends. Why wasn't he bleeding? He should be bleeding.

I sat back and stared at Kheppy.

"What do you think?" she asked.

"I think this card just told me how to prove Ryan was the one who killed Isabelle."

Chapter 25

What Blood?

I DIDN'T EXPECT DETECTIVE Platt to answer when I called him from the car, but I had hoped to speak to a person, not a machine. I needed someone who understood the severity of the situation and who would get a message to the detective, even at this late hour.

No luck, though. There seemed no way around the courteous yet infuriating automated attendant, who kept asking me to leave the information after the beep or call the emergency hotline.

I hung up and considered my options. Was realizing I might have evidence to prove who murdered Isabelle Blake an emergency? I honestly didn't know, so I called someone who would.

Merle answered on the first ring, which told me he hadn't had any better luck getting to sleep tonight than I had. Once I explained what I'd remembered, he urged me to hold tight.

"Leave a message, Boo. The detective is an early bird. He's usually in by seven, and that's only a few hours away. Nothing much can happen before then, anyway."

It was reasonable advice, so I called the detective's number again and left my message after the beep.

"Detective, I think I have DNA evidence that will prove who killed Isabelle. I'm on my way to the shop to get it, and I'll take it to the station when the lobby opens. Please, whatever you do, don't let the mayor transfer Wyatt to the county jail. I can prove he's innocent. He shouldn't be locked up." Especially when he's about to transform into a deadly beast. "Call me back when you get this message, okay? I think that's it. Uh, yeah. All right, then. Bye."

If I wasn't the all-time worst message leaver, I would at least have to be in the top ten. What happened to the good old days when people talked to people instead of machines?

It didn't matter, though. Once the detective got the message, he'd stop Wyatt's transfer. That's what was important.

As I drove to the shop, I spotted an open parking space directly in front. I suppose that was one advantage of coming to work in the middle of the night.

It had been a long time since I'd been here at this hour. The place definitely looked—and felt—different. Maybe it was all the Halloween decorations in the neighboring shop windows—the plastic skeletons and paper ghosts, the fake black cats and crows. But even for someone like me, who adored the holiday, and lived and breathed it all year round, the spooky stuff was still spookier when no one else was around.

The only sign of life on the street appeared to be at the Mexican restaurant almost a full block away, where I could hear the faint strains of a Journey cover tune wafting above the thunder of waves crashing against the shoreline.

The distant blinking neon sign and the dim streetlights offered little help for my tired eyes. Luckily, I knew my shop key well enough to pick it out from the others without a problem, and I slid it into the lock with minimal fumbling.

Once the door was open and I switched on the lights, the creepy-crawly feeling faded. The shop was the same old shop, and it still felt like home.

To my surprise, the merchandise on the shelves had noticeably thinned out since my last visit. Apparently, Sissy was right. We hadn't needed drastic discounts. Score another one for her.

"Hi, Petunia," I said, greeting the witch mannequin as she presided over her cauldron of candy in the shop's window. "Don't mind me. Just here for a little blood."

That sounded more disturbing than I'd intended.

"You're right," I said to my silent friend. "I should stop yapping and get to work."

I examined the white trim around the door, poring over every scratch and scuff, searching for anything that looked like dried blood. My theory was that if Ryan punching the door had bloodied his hand, some of it must have been left behind.

Two dark splotches looked promising, but closer inspection and an unmistakable whiff of chocolate changed my mind. "Sissy's fudge, if I had to guess," I said to the mannequin. "I wouldn't mind some of that fudge right now."

A low growl in my stomach reminded me it had been hours since I'd eaten. I'd gobbled up a small bowl of Del's sausage gumbo before bed, but apparently, my stomach had decided that wasn't enough.

My silent partner maintained her vacant gaze on the cauldron filled with individually wrapped gummy worms and gummy spiders.

I guess I really was hungry because even those rubbery little things looked appetizing. I reached over and took one of the cellophane packages off the top, ripped it, and helped myself to a sugary green worm.

"Not bad," I said as I bit into an orange one. "Better than they look, actually."

I helped myself to a few more packages.

"Okay, that's it," I said to Petunia and the shameful number of empty wrappers crumpled in my hand. How had one package turned into five?

No more, I told myself, or I'd end up with a stomachache.

Before I could lose my resolve, I went to the trash bin tucked beneath the cash register and dropped the wrappers into it. I watched them land on an empty orange soda can and a wad of paper towels.

Wait. Paper towels? Paper towels!

I rushed back to the washroom and grabbed the trash bin there.

Yes! There they were. All the bandage wrappers Sissy had tossed after tending to Ryan's hand, and beneath those was the clump of paper towels I'd remembered.

That big, beautiful clump of bloody paper towels.

Either my excitement over the discovery or all that gummy worm sugar was making my heart pound like a jackhammer in my chest. I leaned against the porcelain sink to catch my breath.

My heart still raced, but everything was fine now, I told myself. The evidence would keep Sissy out of jail. Wyatt would be released before the full moon. Ryan would get what he deserved.

All was finally well.

Good luck telling that to my heart, though. I forced a deep breath, then another.

I had to tell somebody. Once I shared the news, then it would sink in. Then my nerves would settle.

When I fished my phone out of my purse, my finger hovered over Delphine's name. She was always my first call.

But it would also feel good to tell the detective I'd been successful, even if I had to speak to that machine again. I tapped his number and prepared to share the good news.

"Laguna Bay Police Department. Detective Platt speaking."

"What? You're there?" That was not the smoothest way to begin a conversation, but I wasn't expecting him to pick up.

"Yes. Who is this?"

"Sorry. It's Boo. I was going to leave another message. I found it!"

"Found what?"

"The blood. Didn't you get my message?"

"What blood? I just got in. But *what blood*?"

I couldn't blame the guy for sounding panicked. Under the circumstances, I probably should have given him a little more context. "Ryan's blood. He cut his hand at my shop, Sissy patched him up, and the paper towels are still here. You can get DNA from them, right? Then you can match it to the residue you found under Isabelle's fingernails. He's your killer."

"How do you know about the residue? Wait, never mind. How much blood are you talking about? Oh, forget it. We'll take anything. But don't touch it. You don't want to contaminate the sample."

"It's in the trash bin. It's been here since this morning." My triumphant feeling slipped away. Had the evidence already been ruined?

"Did it touch anything in there? Look carefully, but don't touch it."

"Not that I can see. Should I dump it out?"

"No! Don't do anything. I'll grab someone from forensics and come over. It might take a bit to get someone at this hour, but we'll be there as soon as possible. Don't touch the sample!"

"I heard you the first time, Detective. Don't touch it. Got it. Just hurry."

When we hung up, relief flooded through me. For the first time, it felt like this horrible ordeal might be coming to an end.

The *Speed Racer* in my chest was even slowing down. It may be cutting it close—far too close for my liking—but there was still time to get Wyatt home before the full moon. If memory served, a seasoned werewolf could keep himself from transforming until midnight. After that, all bets were off. That gave Wyatt roughly twenty-four hours.

Plenty of time, I hoped.

Gently, I pushed the trash bin back against the wall and glimpsed myself in the mirror. Oh boy. I might feel better, but the woman looking back at me was a mess.

I rarely carried a brush with me, so I used my fingers to coax my misbehaving mane into something more presentable.

I was still in the washroom, wrangling my hair and cleaning away mascara smudges when I heard a noise in the shop.

That detective was quick! Good. The sooner I could get the evidence into his hands, the better.

I checked my hair once more in the mirror, then left the washroom to let him in. Except the darkness outside had turned the shop windows into mirrors, making it impossible to see anything outside. As I made my way toward the door, I searched for the detective and whoever he was bringing to handle the evidence, but all I could see was my reflection.

188

When I reached the door, I cupped my hands to the glass and searched the street. No police cars. No official-looking vehicles at all. Just my little blue Karmann Ghia sitting where I'd parked it.

I stepped back and noticed that the door was unlocked. I must have forgotten to relock it when I entered. I turned the deadbolt and grabbed another package of gummy worms.

"He said it could be a while. Right, Petunia? There are plenty of things that need doing until he gets here." Sissy had already moved some of the costume pieces closer to the front. The ones last-minute shoppers tended to grab, like masks, capes, and fairy wings.

She had also pushed the Halloween door hangings closer together to make room for more plastic jack-o-lanterns near the front. A smart move. As I picked up a package of clown makeup that had been left by the plastic crows to return it to the makeup shelf, I heard another scraping noise. Only this time, it was in the back.

I glanced at Petunia and whispered, "Did you hear that?"

Of course, she hadn't.

"Since when are you a scaredy-cat, Boo?" I scolded myself. "It's an old building. Wood creaks. Pipes rattle. Get over yourself."

Yes, that's what Delphine and Kheppy would say. Or at least what I imagined they would say. I took a deep breath and ventured back into the hallway. It was still dark, which made the light in the washroom even more noticeable.

What caught my eye, however, was the sight of the trash bin tipped over and the bloody paper towels strewn across the floor.

"What in the world..." I wailed as I rushed to the room. Had a stray cat gotten in? A raccoon? An opossum?

Please don't let it be a rat. I really didn't want to deal with a rat infestation on top of everything else.

I threw open the door expecting to shoo away whatever critter had invaded the room, but there was no one. It was the same as I'd left it, except for the overturned trash and a powerful stench of chlorine bleach.

Then, something moving in the mirror caught my attention. I froze. It wasn't something. It was someone, and she was aiming a pistol directly at my head.

Chapter 26
Fateful Reading

"Hurry up," Mallory Haines whispered through gritted teeth as she jabbed the barrel of a shiny pistol into my back. It looked brand new, just like her black velour tracksuit, designer sneakers, and the ball cap she'd pulled low over her still heavily made-up face.

Apparently, criminal activity was no reason to skimp on fashion for Laguna Bay's mayor.

When she dug the barrel in again as I stood at the front door, fumbling with the lock, I told her my fingers were trembling, and the darkness was making it difficult.

What I was really doing was stalling, hoping the detective would show up before Mallory could do whatever she'd come here to do.

"If you would let me leave the light on, it would be a lot easier," I snapped.

She scoffed. "So, someone might come to your rescue? I don't think so. Actually, forget the lock. We're leaving. Get in the car."

When I didn't move, she prodded me again. "Now, Boo."

If I pushed my luck, that dead look in her eye told me she wouldn't hesitate to use that gun. "Why are you doing this, Mallory?"

"You don't get to ask questions," she barked. "Now move it. If you think I'm not serious, just ask Isabelle. Oh wait, you can't. She's dead. Keep this up, Boo, and you'll join her."

That's what I was afraid of. To think I'd tossed Mallory off the suspect list when I learned she and Isabelle had been friends. I guess I had a thing or two to learn about killer motives. I slipped the key in and engaged the deadbolt.

Mallory didn't notice because she was looking up and down the street, as if she could see anything in all this darkness.

I turned around. "Where did you park?"

She laughed. No, it was more of a cackle. "Doesn't matter. We're taking your car."

I couldn't even pretend to fumble with the key again because the broken driver-side window made its locks irrelevant. She waited until I was behind the wheel, then slid into the passenger seat.

As I revved the engine, I turned to her. "C'mon, Mallory. What's this about?"

If I could get her talking, maybe I could convince her to let me go.

She sneered. "We're not playing twenty questions, Boo. Shut up and drive."

"Where do you want to go?"

"Head to the canyon. If you try anything funny, I will shoot you."

"I have no doubt," I muttered and gunned the engine again.

"Then why aren't you moving?"

Because the detective wasn't here yet. I was still hoping someone would come to my rescue. Of course, that's not what I said. "It's an old car. It needs a minute."

That was true in the mornings when the engine was cold or after it sat for a couple of days. Tonight, the engine was still warm from my drive in, but she didn't know that.

She glanced up and down the street, as though she expected someone to approach. Or feared someone might. "That's enough. Go. Now." She pressed the gun's barrel into my thigh to let me know she meant business.

"It's your funeral," I muttered.

"Excuse me?" she asked.

Taunting Mallory when she was holding me at gunpoint probably wasn't the smartest move. I had to control my temper. "This doesn't have to get ugly. I'm sure you have a perfectly rational reason for doing this, so maybe we could start there."

"I don't have to explain myself to you, Boo Boudreaux. You may strut around this town like you own it, but I'm the mayor. You should remember that."

The rise in her voice told me I'd struck a nerve. She was getting so worked up I thought she might not notice the headlights coming toward us as I reached the end of Forest Avenue.

As it grew closer, I could see the outline of police lights straddling the roofline.

Please be the detective. Please be the detective.

It didn't even matter if it was the detective. It could be any officer, anyone with a badge. Even Merle Foster would be a welcome sight.

I prepared to swerve into the vehicle or flash my lights or do something—anything—to get the driver's attention.

Mallory must have sensed it because she jammed that gun so hard into my side, I thought it might have cracked a rib.

"Don't even think about it," she warned. "If you make any suspicious moves, I will shoot you, and Delphine will be next on my list."

That made my blood run cold. Hurting me was one thing. Hurting Delphine was another.

I didn't want to risk my sister's life, but if I worked quickly enough, Mallory could be arrested before she ever made good on that threat.

Unless she had an accomplice. Was that possible?

But then, it didn't matter. The police car passed us, and that fleeting opportunity was gone.

"I knew you were too smart to do something so dumb," she said, obviously pleased with herself. "Get on the canyon road. Head toward your house."

"My sister has nothing to do with this," I said.

"Oh, but she does. You two are thick as thieves. Always have been. Did you know, back when Izzy and I were teens, there was a time we actually idolized you two?"

That was a laugh. "I don't remember you idolizing anyone."

"It's the truth," she added. "You were so cool, so independent. Especially you, Boo. You were the only woman in town with her own shop back then, with no one to answer to but yourself. Back then, my mom told me girls could be nurses, teachers, or homemakers. That was it. When I told her you had your own business, do you know what she said? That you were a witch. That only a witch could tell fortunes like you did. You know what else? She wasn't the only one who called you that."

I'd heard the accusation before, especially around that time. Those Y2K kids had been especially cruel. I could have endured the personal attacks, but once the vandals attacked my shop, breaking windows and spray-painting that hateful moniker over my door, I knew I was risking not just myself, but the whole supernatural community. That's when the Boo-tique was born. A Halloween-themed phoenix that rose from the ashes of my fortune-telling shop.

Mallory had been one of the loudest and cruelest voices during those years. There was even a time I'd believed she and her friends were behind the vandalism, but the police had determined the girls had alibis. Since it had happened so soon after she'd come in for that fateful reading, I still had my doubts.

"People can think whatever they want," I said, struggling to keep that old anger at bay. "It's a free country."

"Why wouldn't you hire us at your shop? Weren't we cool enough for you?"

"Cool enough? Are you serious? You never wanted to work at my shop. You made it clear you thought my shop was a joke, even before you asked for the reading."

The reading that had changed everything.

It hadn't occurred to me before, but the friend who had accompanied Mallory that day must have been Isabelle.

"Maybe I didn't. But Izzy did."

As that old memory became clearer, I could see those two girls in the shop, giggling. Those bright faces with their endless summer tans and freckled noses.

"Do you remember laughing at us?" she asked.

"I did not laugh."

"Oh, you laughed." Pain laced her words.

Yes, I had laughed. But that had been after Mallory's reading, after they had waltzed in like they owned the place, dropped my "help wanted" sign on the counter, and demanded job applications. When I'd asked them about their job experience, knowing full well they didn't have any, Mallory had changed her tune. She slapped money on the counter and demanded a reading.

I know—and I knew that day—I should have refused, but something inside me wanted to put that brat in her place. Let her see what her future holds, I remember thinking. Let her see what this nastiness will get her.

It wasn't my finest hour, and not a day goes by that I don't regret inviting Mallory into my reading parlor and telling her exactly what I saw in the cards.

When I told her someone close to her would cause her great turmoil, she had thought I was simply being mean. It had not gone well. When she accused me of lying, I laughed.

"I laughed," I said, "because I had no reason to lie. You had asked for the reading. It wasn't my fault you didn't like what the cards told you."

"You also laughed at Izzy when she still wanted a job."

"C'mon. You girls weren't serious. Either of you."

"You're wrong, Boo. Izzy needed a job, and you laughed at her. You embarrassed her. You ruined everything that day. Did you know that?"

"I asked two kids to leave my shop. That's all I did." It was such a feeble excuse, but it was true. My instinct was to defend myself, but her clenched jaw and vacant stare warned me not to pursue it.

As much as I didn't enjoy revisiting this painful memory, it gave me an opportunity to ask about something else. "Did you always know Sissy was Isabelle's daughter?"

Mallory shot me a look. "What? No! I had no idea what Izzy did with the baby. I didn't know she even went through with the pregnancy. I thought that was why she left and cut ties with everybody here. But then, she was never the warm and fuzzy type."

Something they had in common, no doubt. As we neared my turnoff, I considered what my chances of survival might be if I took the turn hard enough to flip the car. Or if that was even possible.

Mallory didn't tell me to turn, though. Was she distract-ed? Was my house not the destination?

As we sat in silence, I wondered if I should get her talking again or just let her stew in her anger. The longer she sat, the farther we traveled away from Delphine and Kheppy, and as far as I was concerned, that was a win.

"Take the next right," she said a few moments later.

"Are you sure?" This time, I wasn't trying to stall. I was genuinely surprised.

"Just do it." She pushed the pistol tip into my side again, as if I could forget it was there.

"Fine. I'm turning. Should I keep heading up the hill?"

"Yeah. Up the hill."

She gave me a long, meaningful look. It was now clear she was taking me to Landon Fields.

The only question was—why there?

Chapter 27
Perfect Opportunity

"Get out." Mallory waved the gun toward the door after directing me to pull over and park. We were only halfway up the long driveway to the Landon Fields Art Colony.

But why was she bringing me to the home base for Wyatt's werewolves? Were they partners in crime? Had she killed Isabelle for Wyatt?

I couldn't see the buildings from where we were, but the brightness from the near-full moon at least made it easy to see the eucalyptus trees, sagebrush, and rocky ravines surrounding us.

"Why are we here?" I asked when she came around to my side of the car. Dressed in black from head to toe as she was, she looked more like a shadow than a person. Only the gun glinted in the moonlight.

"Never mind about that. Just go." She jabbed the gun toward the buildings up the hill.

"That way," she barked and pushed me toward the warehouse, not the main building.

"Why?" I asked. "Are we meeting someone? I think I have a right to know."

She made a sound that barely passed for a laugh. When she said, "You'll find out soon enough," her lips twisted into a malicious grin.

Whatever she intended to do here, I wouldn't like it. I knew that much.

Did she plan to kill me? She'd all but admitted to killing Isabelle. And over what? "If you and Isabelle were friends, why did you kill her?"

"We weren't friends," she gasped, her breath heaving from the exertion of climbing the steep driveway. "Not anymore. Friends don't threaten friends."

Imagine that. I had at least two decades on this woman, but she was the one wheezing and heaving. Turns out being on my feet all day at the shop had its advantages.

Maybe if she didn't have that gun, I'd even have a fighting chance of getting away from her.

Or I could distract her.

"Were you fighting over Wyatt?" I asked. "Is that why you threw him in jail?" I didn't actually believe that. But I had to say something, and it was the first thing that sprang to mind.

"You have quite an imagination, old lady."

That was just mean. On the bright side, I must have rankled her. Maybe enough for her to get sloppy and make a mistake.

"I couldn't care less about that jerk," she groused. "But maybe it was his fault too. Yours and his."

"What was our fault?" I asked.

We were still walking, and she was still heaving. Then she stopped and aimed the gun at my chest. "You really want to know?"

"Isn't that why you brought me out here? To tell me?"

She laughed that cackling laugh again. "No, that's not why we're here. But I'll tell you anyway, because this is where everything went wrong. Right here."

"At Landon Fields?" What did she have to do with this place? What did *I* have to do with this place?

But Mallory wasn't paying attention to me anymore. She wasn't even aiming that stupid gun at me. She was staring at the old eucalyptus tree standing at the bend.

"Right here, Boo. That woman was standing right here. It was so dark, and she was in the shadows. How was I supposed to see her? I wouldn't even have been here if it weren't for Izzy. And she wouldn't have been here either if you hadn't laughed at her that day. She wouldn't have been upset, and she wouldn't have said yes when Wyatt asked us to come up here and spiked our drinks with his dad's liquor. We wouldn't have..." She swallowed hard. "I never even saw that woman until..."

The contours of Mallory's face were lost in the shadows, but the moonlight shimmered on the tears streaming down her cheeks. That's when I knew.

"The girl who died here. That was because of you?"

Mallory wiped her hand across her face. "No, Boo. Haven't you been listening? It was you and Wyatt and Izzy. You know, I was actually glad when she left town. It made it easier. We promised each other never to tell anyone, and then she was gone. It was like it never happened."

I could see where this was going. "But then she came back. Did it bring back the guilt?"

Mallory half-laughed. "She was going to tell. After all these years, she was going to tell the police what had happened that night. Do you know why? She had cancer. She was dying. Before she went, she wanted to clear her conscience, and she wanted to get Sissy away from you. Oh, she hated that Sissy was under your thumb. Her own daughter. When she found out Sissy was working for you, she said she was going to do whatever it took to ruin you. It was her idea to send the code enforcers to your shop. She knew they'd find some violation. And if you had to compete with another Halloween store, we both knew you wouldn't stand a chance."

I'd been right. That vendetta against me had been personal. It wasn't much of a consolation, though.

"So, you killed her because she was going to ruin you too?"

She kept the gun aimed at me. "It all happened so perfectly. Like it was meant to be. I was going to visit Izzy's shop early to let her know when to expect the judges, so she'd be sure to have everything ready, but I saw her crossing the street to your shop. I wanted to stop her from doing something foolish, but by the time I parked and walked back, it was too late. I saw them arguing through the window, Izzy and Sissy's boyfriend. He pushed her and then he ran out the door. He didn't even look back, so he never saw me go inside. She'd hit her head on the cauldron. She should have died."

"But she didn't."

"She should have," Mallory repeated. "But don't you see? It was a perfect opportunity. I could make it all go away."

"But you killed your friend."

"She was dying anyway."

Mallory was not only a killer, she felt absolutely no remorse.

I might have tried to run, test my luck at getting away from this lunatic, but a twig cracked in the distance, behind a rocky outcrop. Mallory and I both turned to search the darkness. Then another twig snapped farther down the hill, and fear licked my spine.

Someone, or something, was stalking us.

"Who's there?" I yelled, hoping the predator couldn't hear the tremble in my voice.

A soft breeze rustled the leaves, and my heart thundered in my ears.

"Do you think it's a mountain lion?" Mallory asked, holding the gun now with both hands and aiming at anything that moved. "They venture into this part of the canyon to hunt, don't they?"

"It's definitely not a mountain lion," I said. Even though it was a clever cover story for the real predators in the area.

"What do you think it is?"

How could I tell her I knew exactly what it was, and it was far worse than a mountain lion?

Then the wolf howled, and I didn't have to say a word. She squared herself at that feral cry and aimed, ready to shoot whatever came at us.

Then, that single wolf's cry was joined by a whole chorus. Five? Six? Ten? It was impossible to know.

One thing was certain—we didn't stand a chance.

"Run!" I yelled at her. "Run!"

Chapter 28

Terrifying Feline

MALLORY DIDN'T ARGUE. SHE scrambled along the gravel after me. Fear drove us both up the last stretch of the Landon Fields driveway.

"This way," she screamed, motioning for me to follow her to the warehouse. I was headed for the main house, but she was right. Darren Landon and the other residents would only be there if they weren't the wild beasts hunting us down.

But Mallory didn't know about the werewolves. Did she? Why would she think it would be safer in the warehouse?

There wasn't time to question her, though. I could see movement along the lane. Two wolves—no, three—flanked us on that side. More of them approached from the other side.

"Over here, Boo. Help me." Mallory was struggling to open the warehouse's double metal doors. She didn't need to know they were werewolves to know they couldn't open a door.

We'd be safer inside.

She pulled the extra-large barrel slide bolt that kept the doors shut and waved me inside. "Get in. Hurry."

I did, and she pulled the doors closed behind us.

Relief washed over me once she found a switch that turned on the overhead lights. I leaned against a post and caught my breath. "That was close."

Mallory paced the floor, between the glass-heating furnace and an enormous worktable a few steps away. She paused at the table and studied the artists' tools scattered across it. Then she pulled a paper towel from her pocket and rubbed it along the iron shaft used to blow glass.

When had she donned that pair of latex gloves? I was about to ask when she turned around. One look at her ice-cold expression was enough to silence me.

The shaft was twice as long as a baseball bat, but that didn't stop Mallory from gripping it like a batter waiting at the plate.

"What are you doing?" It seemed clear she intended to whack me with it, which meant I had to get her talking again. It was my only defense until I found something I could use to protect myself.

"Why are you doing this?" I pressed when she didn't respond. To think I thought I was safer here. "I don't care why you killed Isabelle. Let me go, and your secret will be safe with me."

She rounded the corner of the table and came toward me. "Do you think I'm that stupid? You would never do that. Luckily, you won't have a chance to tell anyone anything."

"This is insane." I backed away, trying to keep a safe distance between me and the deadly end of that iron rod. "You'll never get away with it." As I shuffled backward again, I nearly tripped over a low wooden stool.

"Of course I will." She let out a cynical, hateful chuckle. "I won't be anywhere near this crime scene when the police find you, and when they do discover you, that young man's blood is going to be all over the murder weapon. It'll paint an obvious story for the authorities. He killed you to stop you from turning him in, and he brought you here to frame Wyatt's family for his crime."

Is that the alibi she'd cooked up for herself? She was going to kill me and frame Ryan?

Another nasty laugh gurgled out of her.

"It'll be an open-and-shut case, Boo. No muss, no fuss. It's kind of brilliant, if I say so myself."

She was always the first to congratulate herself. "You might be right, Mallory, but why go to all this trouble? I was already accusing Ryan of Isabelle's murder. You didn't have to do any of this."

She choked up on that giant iron rod and swung it at me. Too far to hit, but close enough to taunt. "If only that were true. The evidence the coroner found on Isabelle won't match that young man's DNA. But if the authorities think he killed you to cover up Isabelle's murder, it won't matter. They'll know he's guilty."

"But he isn't guilty."

She scoffed. "They don't know that."

I tried to think of a way to keep the conversation going. My mind raced, but then something scratched at the door.

Fingernails on a chalkboard had nothing on the sound of wolf's claws scraping over metal. I winced at the agony of it. Then the clawing became barking, punctuated by low moans, growls, and howls.

Mallory tensed as she listened. "They can't get in. I secured the door."

Outside, the wolves went silent.

"See?" she asked. "They already gave up."

I wasn't so sure. Then something thudded along the back wall. A door swung open, and a stream of husky wolves rushed inside and fanned out. Some jumped on top of the metal cabinets along the wall. Others crouched low around us. They moved so quickly, they had us surrounded before I could move.

Not that there was anywhere to go. That locked door had been our only defense. I should have known there would be another way in.

As the rest of the pack entered, they formed a circle around us.

Mallory had dropped the shaft back on the table and had grabbed her gun again. She aimed it at the closest wolf, a silvery creature with black ears and black eyes. With no better weapon to defend myself, I grabbed the iron rod she'd discarded. I tried to wield it as she had, but the stupid thing was so heavy. It was all I could do to keep it upright.

"If we work together, I think we can fend them off," I said, backing toward her. I envisioned us working in tandem, like fighting duos in the movies.

"I'm not saving you. You're on your own." She darted toward the open back door.

"Wait!" I panicked and tried to swing the massive rod at the three wolves advancing on me.

A gunshot rattled my brain. When I looked over my shoulder, I saw her aiming at a wolf standing between her and the door. She must have missed because the animal leaped out of the way, and she ran for the opening.

I did the same. I put everything I had into that mad dash. But when I glanced back to see if we were in the clear, I didn't realize she had stopped. I crashed into her back, which sent us both tumbling to the floor.

I scrambled back to my feet and saw what had brought her to a halt. An animal blocked the door. It wasn't a wolf, and it didn't look like any mountain lion I'd ever seen.

The menacing feline was three times the size of a mountain lion, gray and black with two startlingly white front paws. Its tawny eyes burned like flames.

"Is that a...?" Mallory whispered, too awestruck to finish the question.

"A tiger? Yeah, that's a tiger," I said, finishing it for her. It seemed impossible. How was this exotic animal running around the foothills of Laguna Bay?

I didn't have a clue, but there it was, staring at us.

Mallory aimed her gun at the animal's sizable head. I waited for her to shoot. It should have been easy to hit the creature from this distance. But Mallory didn't pull the trigger. Then her arms—and her aim—lowered to the floor.

"I'm not moving my arms." Her voice verged on hysterical. "Something else is controlling me."

The stress had clearly gotten to the woman. Once the gun aimed downward, her hands unclasped and dropped to her sides. The gun dangled loosely in her right hand.

"Mallory, what are you doing?" I didn't want her to hurt the animal, but I was pretty sure the iron rod was no match for those claws or those fangs.

When she didn't respond, I waved my hand in front of her face.

She didn't flinch. Nobody was home.

"Mallory!" I shook her shoulder. Still nothing.

She will be all right, and she will no longer hurt you. She will no longer hurt anyone.

I whipped around. Where had that voice come from? Because it sounded like it was in my head. And it sounded like...

It is I, Lucille.

"Don't call me that," I snapped as the realization hit me. This was Kheppy. But how?

A low whimper behind me reminded me we weren't alone. I whipped around to see the whole wolf pack gathered behind me. They could have torn me apart if they had wanted to, but they all sat as still and silent as Mallory, transfixed by the tiger-sized Kheppy sitting in the doorway.

Then the largest one, the silvery one who had led the others, turned its attention to me and stepped forward. His head lowered, his shoulders hunched forward, and his limbs and spine jerked and twitched in unnatural ways.

As he writhed in what looked like agonizing pain, my instinct was to go to him. To offer comfort, even if I didn't know the first thing about comforting a werewolf.

Do not approach him.

It was that voice in my head again. Kheppy's voice.

This is their way.

I did what she said and held back.

The transformation took less than a minute, but that minute felt like an hour—an excruciating hour. At the end of it, Darren stood before us in nothing but his birthday suit. The young man at least had the decency to turn away.

I handed him a leather apron hanging from a nearby hook, so he could cover himself.

When he appeared uninterested in doing so, I thrust the apron more forcefully. "Please, Mr. Landon. It will make you more comfortable."

He looked back at his canine friends and laughed. "I think you mean it will make you more comfortable."

I wasn't going to quibble.

Once the apron was on, he grabbed a coiled rope from the wall, took Mallory's gun, set it on the table, and bound her wrists behind her back.

"There," he said. "Will you call her off now?"

"Pardon me?" I wasn't sure he was speaking to me, but Mallory was still in her strangely catatonic state. "Call off who?"

Darren jutted his chin at Kheppy, who was still blocking the door. Still watching everything.

"She does not control me, hound."

For a second, I thought it was Kheppy's voice in my head, but no. Darren had heard it. They all had.

"We weren't going to hurt you, Boo. We could smell the guilt on this one." He jerked her shoulder, which elicited no response from Mallory.

"Were you going to stop her from hurting me?" Had they meant to help me?

"No, Boo," Kheppy answered for him. "They did not intend to help you. Only to stop this woman from getting away. They intended only to save themselves. Scratching their own backs, as you say."

The mangled meaning made me cringe a little, but I wasn't about to correct a five-hundred-pound cat. I turned to the far less threatening Darren. "Is that true?"

"We could have hurt you if that was our intention. That should be proof enough."

I wasn't sure I believed him, but it was probably better to let it go.

Kheppy seemed to agree. She sauntered closer to Darren, which made him visibly tense. "I will hold you to your word, hound."

"Fine, I'm not lying."

She eyed him for another moment, then her gaze slid to his companions. The wolves closest to us bowed their heads. Those in the back, who had risen to their feet, shuffled backward. "We shall see."

As Kheppy turned to leave through the back door, she paused and turned back to me. "I will tell Delphine where you are. I will tell her you are safe." Then she glanced again at Darren as if daring him to contradict her.

When he didn't, she took off, out into the darkness, leaving me alone with a still unresponsive Mallory and an uneasy truce with the werewolves.

As I watched her disappear in a blur of stripes and moonlight, all I could think was—my cat just turned into a tiger, and somehow that wasn't even the scariest thing to happen tonight.

Chapter 29
Two Conditions

"I'm telling you, Detective, a pack of wolves chased us into that warehouse, and they weren't just wolves." Mallory paused, glanced around, and leaned closer to Detective Platt. "They were *werewolves*."

I watched our town's mayor, looking as unlike her official self as I'd ever seen her, with her ball cap barely containing her now loose and tangled hair and muddy streaks soiling her designer tracksuit, trying to explain the night's chaos. I couldn't help but feel sorry for the detective. As Mallory became increasingly agitated, he stared at his notepad and rubbed his lower lip, trying to hide his confusion and disbelief.

The night sky faded to a hazy gray while I sat on the bumper of the ambulance—equal parts exhausted and vaguely amused—waiting for my turn to be questioned. Darren had called the emergency hotline, and now we had the full parade: patrol cars, a fire engine, and more flashing lights than a Fourth of July block party.

Mallory had shaken off her trancelike state soon after Kheppy left. By the time the first responders arrived, the woman was back in boss mode and insisted on speaking to the detective first. I was happy to step back and eavesdrop on her account.

She'd remembered more from that hypnosis—or whatever it was—than I would have thought.

"Werewolves? What makes you say that, Madam Mayor?" The detective's lip twitched again.

"He changed right in front of me." She pointed at Darren, who was standing with an officer a few paces away answering questions. "Transformed or shifted or whatever you call it."

Darren must have overheard her, too, because he glanced at her mid-answer, chuckled, and shook his head. The officer standing beside him chuckled as well.

Good. If no one took her seriously, our supernatural community might actually survive.

As angry as the wolves were, even they didn't want to lose their home.

None of us did.

"Boo! Boo! Where's Boo?"

I craned my head around the side of the ambulance and spotted my sister, then waved to catch her attention.

She hurried over, but she wasn't alone. Cradled tightly in her arms was Kheppy. Back to her ordinary size and looking as annoyed as ever to be locked in that embrace.

I would have asked Kheppy if she'd shared the night's adventure with Delphine, but Merle was with them. Even if the cat was ready to reveal her long-held secrets to other supernaturals, I wanted to find out why she'd been keeping this tiger-sized secret from us before we shared it with anyone else.

Delphine was so flushed and out of breath when she reached me, I scooted over to give her room on the bumper to sit, so the poor thing could settle and rest. It didn't stop her from peppering me with questions while she kept her grip on Kheppy. "Are you all right? Are you hurt?"

"I'm fine. Not a scratch." I reached over to pet the cat between the ears. "Thanks to Kheppy here." I lowered my voice to a whisper so no one else could hear. "Did she tell you what happened?"

Delphine looked down at the cat and whispered back. "She told me we needed to get here quickly. She said you would explain. Was it Wyatt's son? Is he behind all this?"

Two EMTs approached, and one of them climbed past me into the back of the ambulance. "Excuse me, ma'am."

I moved to give him room.

"Actually, no. It was Mallory. She killed Isabelle and planned to kill me, too, then frame Ryan for both murders. Darren stopped her, with some help."

Kheppy gave a grumbly harrumph, letting me know that wasn't exactly her recollection.

"That's the story we're going with, at least for now," I whispered to her.

Delphine sighed and smiled in understanding.

Merle, however, looked more worried than ever.

I touched his hand. "I'm fine. Truly. Just a little rattled."

"No thanks to me." He pulled his cowboy hat off his head and held it to his chest. "It's my fault. I nearly got you killed, Boo. Me and my big mouth."

Delphine sensed the conversation had taken a troublesome turn. She rose and hugged Kheppy. "I'm going to check with the other residents. See if they need any help with anything, or..." She hurried off without even finishing the sentence.

I turned every ounce of my attention to Merle. "What do you mean? What did you do?"

He stared at his brim as he slid it through his fingers. "After you called me, I called the mayor. I thought I was helping. I told her to stop Wyatt's transfer because you had proof he was innocent. She wanted to know what it was. It seemed a reasonable request. I thought she just wanted to know it was solid evidence."

"You told her I suspected Ryan? You told her his blood was at the shop?" That's how she knew. That's why she'd ambushed me.

He nodded. "After I told her, she said she'd square things up with Wyatt right away. I never in a million years thought I was putting you in danger, but that's exactly what I did."

He glanced to his right and frowned at what appeared to be empty space to anyone else, but I knew better. "You don't think I know that? I know you said I shouldn't trust her. But she's the mayor, and you're not always right."

"Merle?" I interrupted his conversation with Rupert because the technician was still inside the cab.

"Right," he muttered and stared at his fingers. "We'll finish this later."

"I'm all right." I touched his hand again so anyone who might have overheard him would think he'd been speaking to me.

"Do you forgive me?" he asked.

"Of course. You were trying to help. I would never be angry with you for that."

It was an innocent mistake, and I'd certainly made my share of those. I was ready to accuse Ryan Stokes of a murder he didn't commit because I'd misread a stupid tarot card. All these years, I'd blamed the cards for Mallory's disastrous reading. But the fault was my own, just as it had been last night. If the cards were, as Kheppy said, a reflection of our own intuition, mine was in dire need of an adjustment.

But that was a problem for another day.

A few paces away, Delphine was watching the detective step away from the mayor to take a phone call. Kheppy was, too, and when the mayor backed away from the detective toward the open driver's-side door of an empty squad car, the cat slipped out of Delphine's grip, darted toward Mallory, and leaped onto her chest.

"What? Hey! Get this animal off me. Ow!" Mallory pushed and did everything she could to dislodge Kheppy, without success.

When Detective Platt turned to see the commotion, he rushed to help. Only he didn't go for the cat. In the time it took him to cover three long strides, he slipped his phone into a pocket, pulled a pair of handcuffs from another pocket and grabbed one of Mallory's hands as she tried to wrangle Kheppy off her.

"What are you doing?" Mallory demanded when he slapped the handcuffs around her wrist. "I'm being attacked."

As soon as the metal lock latched, Kheppy jumped to the ground and strutted back toward Delphine and me.

The detective ignored the mayor and grabbed her other hand behind her back. "Madam Mayor, that was the coroner. He has tested your DNA against a sample we collected from the Boo-tique victim's body, and it's a match. You are under arrest for the murder of Isabelle Blake."

That set off an angry tirade of expletives that made even the detective blush. Still, the man maneuvered Mallory into the back of the squad car, then huddled with another officer, who slid into the driver's seat. With a couple *of whoop-whoops* of the siren, the other emergency folks and artist colony residents cleared a path so the car could leave.

"So, is that the end of it?" Merle asked the detective, who had joined us beside the ambulance.

"I think so, Mr. Foster. The DNA evidence is pretty conclusive, but unless the mayor confesses, it will be up to a jury to decide. I'm still not exactly clear on what happened here, though." He scratched the top of his head, Columbo-style. "The mayor seemed fuzzy on how she ended up here tonight, but Darren Landon says she brought you here to kill you and frame Ryan Stokes by making it look like he was trying to frame the Landons. Is that your understanding, ma'am?"

Merle stepped forward. "It's been a traumatic night, Detective. Could we do this later?"

"No, Merle," I said. "It's all right. Detective, yes. I believe that's what happened. She attacked me in my shop right after I called you."

He nodded, as if I were confirming his suspicions. "And there's one more thing. I've been looking around, and I can identify canine paw prints. Were you really chased by a pack of wolves, like the mayor said?"

I'd heard her say werewolves, but he conveniently left that out. Across the gravel parking lot, I saw Darren watching me.

"I can't help you there, Detective. My memory is pretty fuzzy." I didn't like deceiving him, but I didn't want the police searching for a violent pack of wolves, either.

Darren approached us. "Did I hear you say something about wolves, Detective?" He pulled something out of his back pocket. When he held out the hairy rubber mask, I noticed it was part of the costume he'd purchased in my shop. "I was trying out my mask before any trick-or-treaters come around tonight. Maybe she saw me."

The detective pulled out his notepad and made a note. "I suppose it's possible. It wouldn't be the strangest thing to happen during a full moon, and it is Halloween. She probably saw some costumes, and her imagination ran wild."

I nodded. "Sounds like a reasonable explanation to me."

"Could I borrow that mask, Mr. Landon?" the detective asked. "I should log it as evidence."

"Sure," Darren said. "The officer I was just speaking to said the department is dropping the charges against my father. Does that mean I can bring him home?"

"It sure does." The detective produced a plastic bag and slipped the mask inside. "The paperwork needs a few signatures, but he should be cleared for release by noon."

"I'm happy to hear you say that," Darren said.

"It's the least we can do." The detective waved over a uniformed officer and gave him instructions to return the bag to the station. When the officer left, the detective turned to Darren. "I hope you know we were acting on the best information we had at the time. I'm sorry we got it wrong."

For a second, I thought Darren would say something snide. Instead, he said, "We just want him back as soon as possible," and walked away.

"I suppose that went about as well as it could have," the detective said to Merle and me.

He had no idea how true that was. If Wyatt's release had been delayed any longer, it would have been a much different—and far more unpleasant—conversation.

Merle moved up closer to the detective. "Say, are you going to need Boo for anything else, or can I get her out of here?"

Detective Platt pulled out his notepad and flipped through a few pages. "I think I've got enough for the report, but I might have some follow-up questions. May I contact you later today?"

"Could it wait till tomorrow?" I asked. "Today is Halloween, and it'll be a busy day at the shop, plus the trick-or-treating tonight. I just love seeing all the children dressed up in their costumes."

"Understood," the detective said. "Tomorrow will be fine. Go on. Enjoy the day, but I suggest getting some rest first. It's been a long night."

"Thanks, Detective," Merle said and shook the man's hand. "I'll keep an eye on her."

After Detective Platt walked away, I hopped off the ambulance bumper. "Merle, I'm fully capable of deciding whether I need to rest. I can take care of myself."

He turned to me with a sad smile. "Will you ever let me help you? I almost lost you today, and I don't know what I'd do if that happened. Please let me do this."

I thought I was reading too much into what he said, but then I saw the girlish smile on Delphine's face. A few decades ago, she might have hummed the "first comes love" children's ditty to make her point.

We were decades past that kind of teasing, but her smile said it all.

"All right, Merle. You can help. But you can't stop me from going to the shop."

He frowned and prepared to argue with me.

I held up my hand to stop him. "It's Halloween, and I will go to the Boo-tique. I want to be sure we're ready

222

for the trick-or-treaters and check on Sissy. I hope Ryan is there, too, because I owe him an apology."

"Why? He didn't even know what Mallory was up to."

"I nearly accused him of a murder he didn't commit."

"The DNA from those bloody paper towels never would have implicated him," Merle said.

"I still believe an apology is in order." It was simply the right thing to do.

"Fair point," he said. "I'll take you to the shop on two conditions."

"Who said this was a negotiation?" I snapped back. After the sharp look he gave me, I added, "What are the conditions?"

"First," he said, taking both of my hands in his own. "Well, it's not really a condition. It's more me coming clean about something."

I braced for another dose of bad news.

"I wasn't completely honest when I told you about that last-minute mayoral candidate. It's me, Boo. I plan to file the paperwork on Monday, but only if you think it's a good idea. I think I could be a good mayor for this town, for all residents, not just our own—"

He winced when I put up my hand to stop him. I rushed to explain. "You don't need to convince me. You would make a wonderful mayor, certainly better than, well, you know."

"Do you really think so?"

"I do. Let me know how I can help. Whatever you need. You can count on me."

"You have no idea how much that means to me. Thank you, Boo."

"You said you had two conditions?"

He took a deep breath and clasped both of my hands in his. "I know I messed things up between us all those years ago. But I'd like the opportunity to make it up to you. I'd like a second chance."

I didn't know I'd been waiting to hear those words until that moment. And on this day, of all days. My absolute favorite day of the year.

"Yes, Merle Foster," I said. "I would like that. Very much."

His lips spread into a happy yet hesitant smile. "That's not a trick, is it? I don't think my heart could take it."

"No tricks. Honest."

He pulled my fingers up to his lips and kissed them. "Then that's the only treat I need."

I leaned against his chest, which still felt so familiar after all these years. "Me too," I murmured, just as a chuckle rumbled in his chest. I pulled back. "What's so funny?"

He was trying to keep a straight face. "I was just thinking, since it's Halloween, does this make you my ghoul-friend?"

———

Boo, Kheppy, and the rest of the Laguna Bay gang will be back soon to solve new mysteries. Find the latest updates at https://DeAnnaDrake.com, but keep reading to enjoy a special bonus recipe included in this edition.

Bonus Recipe: Boo's Favorite Lemon Curd Cupcakes with Lemon Buttercream Frosting

LEMON CURD CUPCAKES

Yield: 12 cupcakes | Prep Time: 20 minutes | Bake Time: 18-20 minutes

Ingredients:

- 1 1/2 cups all-purpose flour

- 1 1/2 tsp baking powder

- 1/4 tsp salt

- 1/2 cup unsalted butter, softened

- 1 cup granulated sugar

- 2 large eggs

- 2 tsp vanilla extract

- 2 Tbsp lemon zest (about 2 lemons)

- 1/2 cup whole milk

- 2 Tbsp fresh lemon juice

- 1 cup prepared lemon curd (store-bought or homemade)

Instructions:

Preheat oven to 350°F (175°C). Line a 12-cup muffin tin with paper liners.

In a bowl, whisk flour, baking powder, and salt. In a large mixing bowl, cream the butter and sugar until light and fluffy. Beat in eggs one at a time, then add vanilla and lemon zest. Mix in lemon juice and milk, alternating with dry ingredients until just combined. Divide the batter evenly among the liners, filling about two-thirds full. Bake 18–20minutes, or until a toothpick comes out clean. Cool completely.

Once the cupcakes are cool, use a small knife or cupcake corer to remove the center (about the size of a teaspoon).

Fill each with a spoonful of lemon curd. Replace some or all of the removed portion of the cake on top.

Serving tip: These taste best slightly chilled, so the lemon curd is cool and refreshing against the soft cake.

—ele—

LEMON BUTTERCREAM FROSTING

Yield: Enough for 12–14 cupcakes

—ele—

Ingredients:

- 1 cup unsalted butter, softened

- 3 1/2 cups powdered sugar, sifted

- 3 Tbsp lemon juice

- 1 tsp lemon zest

- Pinch of salt

- 1–2 Tbsp heavy cream (as needed for consistency)

Instructions:

Beat the butter until creamy. Add powdered sugar gradually, then lemon juice, zest, and salt. Add cream a little at a time until fluffy and spreadable. To decorate, pipe or spread frosting on each cupcake. Garnish with a twist of lemon zest, candied lemon peel, or a small edible flower for a charming touch.

Free Novella (Subscriber Exclusive)

GRAB *DEAD END DATE*, a free novella available exclusively to members of my Cozy Mystery Readers Club. The book is part of the Purr-fect Relic series, which is where Boo and Khepeset first made their debut. Within its pages you'll discover how Rebecca and Khepeset's sister, Aneksi, hunt down another killer during Rebecca's first date with Detective Nick Devon at Citrus Grove's hottest new nightspot. *Dead End Date* can be read as a stand-alone story, but it fits chronologically between *Paws, Claws, and Curses* and *Hisses, Hexes, and Homicide*.

When you join me and other cozy mystery readers in the Cozy Mystery Readers Club, you'll also have access to free puzzles, book-related recipes, behind-the-scenes tidbits, and other bonus content. Sign up at DeAnnaDrake.com/join. It's free and easy, and you won't miss any of the fun!

Dear Reader

THANK YOU FOR TAKING the time to read *Candy, Cauldrons, and a Corpse*, the first book in the Laguna Bay Midlife Witch Cozy Mystery series. It's such a joy to share the adventures — and misadventures — of these new Laguna Bay characters, who live just a hop, skip, and a jump away from Rebecca, Aneksi, and the rest of the Citrus Grove gang in the Purr-fect Relic Cozy Mysteries.

If they've earned a soft spot in your book-loving heart, it would mean so much to me if you could jot a few words in a review at your favorite retailer. Good reviews and positive word of mouth are extremely helpful to an author and always deeply appreciated.

Books by DeAnna Drake and Author's Other Work

LAGUNA BAY MIDLIFE WITCH COZY MYSTERY SERIES

Candy, Cauldrons, and a Corpse

A WORLD OF MAGICAL CATS RELIC COZY MYSTERY SERIES

Trouble at the Christmas Tea (novella)

A PURR-FECT RELIC COZY MYSTERY SERIES

Paws, Claws, and Curses
Dead End Date (novella)
Hisses, Hexes, and Homicide
Furballs and Felonies
Crime and Cat-astrophes

Blackmail and Kitty Tails
Whiskers and Ciphers

A MAGICAL MOUSE CAPER SERIES

Mouse in the House

FANTASY FICTION
WRITTEN AS D.D. CROIX

THE QUEEN'S FAYTE SERIES

Memory Thief (prequel story)
Dragonfly Maid
Slivering Curse
Shadow Rite
Guardian of the Realm

ele

HISTORICAL AND CONTEMPORARY ROMANCE WRITTEN AS DEANNA CAMERON

THE DANCER CHRONICLES

The Girl on the Midway Stage
The Girl on the Vaudeville Stage

CALIFORNIA BELLY DANCE ROMANCE SERIES

Shimmy for Me
Dance with Me
Jingly Bells

About DeAnna Drake

DEANNA DRAKE IS AN award-winning author who writes witty and whimsical cozy mysteries filled with magical animals and feisty heroines who are always striving to balance the scales of justice in an offbeat world.

Under different names, DeAnna writes young-adult fantasy fiction, contemporary romances, and historical novels set in the Victorian and Edwardian eras.

When she isn't plotting new adventures for her characters, she's usually planning her next afternoon tea, binging crime shows, and escaping to Disneyland whenever she can.

She lives in Southern California with her family, which includes her two favorite people and one ridiculously pampered border collie. Learn more at https://DeAnna Drake.com.

Or connect on social media:
Facebook:
https://www.facebook.com/DeAnnaDrakeWrites
Instagram:
https://www.instagram.com/deannadrakeauthor